"Cocktail for Disaster"

Part 1

Disclaimer

This book is a work of fiction. Any similarities to persons, places or events are purely coincidental. I have worked on this book; which will be a two part series for many, many years now. I have tried to remain true to the development of the characters, in how they would interact, and converse with one another. If any of the information contained therein offends you, let me apologize beforehand but as you realize it is impossible to please everyone. I hope you can look beyond taking anything offensively, to enjoy a good read.

That being said writing is an escape; it is for enjoyment. It also serves the purpose of getting messages to your audience. It is through these pages, and characters that I hope I capture your attention to a bigger picture here, and bring about some awareness of potential dangers still out there, yet be entertaining..

We are almost on to the best part…"Cocktail for Disaster"
Happy Reading!

Acknowledgements

Praise be to God always. He has given me a gift, and has molded and guided me into perfecting this talent so that I am able to share it with the world. It has been a long time coming since this second book. I had to take a mental break from writing, and people I love to get things back in perspective. Thank God for clarity. I have returned. The road to success takes a lot of hard work and dedication, sometimes we get impatient with the process and choose to cut corners, but that does not get you to your destination any quicker. God is in no hurry to rush along the blessings he has planned for your life. Take time and enjoy the little things, do not always wait for that "big" moment or you may miss what is working in your life right now.

As you can see, God is a major influence. He is number one. I do have other honorable mentions to give or heartfelt thanks to my other influences, which are my dear family and friends (too many to name). Whether I have talked to you yesterday, or a year ago, you know who you are. They are the ones who believed in me with no malice in their heart, and who always told me what was right, if I wanted to hear it or not. They were the ones pushing to continue with my goals, when I had long given up on my dreams. They, in being a friend know that I wish to be an even better friend in return. If this sounds like you, and it is with a pure heart that you wish these good things upon my life, then I am speaking to you! I would not be where I am today without you. There are not enough words or time to express my gratitude and humility. You all are awesome.

Kaylah, my daughter, I pray that I have given you hope and the tools you need to make your mark on the world. Everyone is capable of greatness, and it is up to you to find out where your greatness lies. I hope as your mother, I have set a good example of footsteps to follow in, not to mirror, but pointing you in the right direction to fulfill your destiny. I can't wait to see the wonderful woman you'll become. I love you.

A special thanks goes to Karim C. for assisting with the book cover design, you rock! Next, would like to thank Timothy M, for his poem "What I would like" communicated from Terrence's standpoint, and Noxie Studio Photography for my photo shoots and website maintenance.

Lastly, I dedicate this book to my brother Leroy Woods, I miss you dearly bro, but you have guided me through every step of this process even in your absence. I love you.

Family and Friends, I leave you with this. It is an inspirational quote from an unknown source. *"Life is like a Camera...**Focus** on what's important, **Capture** the good times, **Develop** from the negatives, and if things don't work out, **Take another shot.**"*

"Cocktail for Disaster"

Part 1

1

Tamika was finished bringing the last of her storage boxes off the loading van. She tipped the two movers she had hired for their assistance as she met them in the lobby, and thanked them for their services; but the bulk of the hard labor she handled herself. She didn't have to but that's just who she had become Ms. Independent, and Self-Sufficient.

Re-entering her new spot her mind wandered on how it was a long and exhausting week, trying to move her belongings into her newly cemented piece of real estate and in all the disarray still make it in to work in the mornings. Her boss was gracious enough to let her leave at noon and tomorrow she can awaken at her discretion since she has Friday off. Now standing in the middle of what is soon to be her tidy, newly furnished one-bedroom condominium she smiled to herself, and said, "I have finally gotten myself together!"

As she was savoring the moment of solitude, just then her cell phone rang; she looked at the Caller I.D. and said "drama". She sent the call straight to voicemail. It was Ann and right now, she did not have the time nor energy to listen to her go on about her cheating man. Mentally exhausted from her situations, and trying to move forward, she wondered why Ann could not do the same thing.

"I didn't even answer the call and I am still making the girl's problems mine." Taking a deep breath, surveying the room, she thought, "Now where do I begin?" That answer no easier than deciding that Brooklyn instead of Harlem was where she was going to live.

Tamika saw a box marked "Masterpieces" and decided to go with that one. It was her life's work in there, writings dating all the way back to Junior High School. Yes, Tamika was quite talented with the gift of word, she envisioned once Oprah got wind of her, her dreams would finally be a reality, but until then she would keep adding to her collection. Opening the box with the scissors from the back pocket of her Overalls, she took out a notebook, and pen, leaned against the wall, and slid down to the floor. The wheels of creativity were turning, and with that she begun "My Life as Only I know It"

You want to tell me who you think I am,
When nothing could be further from the truth,
As your "definition" of me
Lacks so many levels of accuracy,
I will let you know when,
If the day ever comes that you say something about me that is true,
I suggest if you want to throw stones, then the person you should look at,
Should definitely start with <u>YOU!</u>

2

"No, No, No, it's all wrong man!" I can't go onstage and perform that, I'll get booed! That was Terrence talking to his homeboys Anthony and Dre. He was going over some new material that he had written for an upcoming show, and as usual, he asked for his homeboys' opinion, but when they give it to him, he doesn't respect it anyway. So every few days, or whenever they saw each other, this is their ritual.

"What do you think?" Terrence would ask.

"Good" they would reply, and then Terrence would say "Nah, I know I can come better than that."

"Look", you stay here in BBQ's and come better than that if you want to, now standing, and placing money on the table for the tab; Ant motioned "I'm out."

As far as I'm concerned, our workday is complete, now it's time to unwind and socialize. I'm going to head over to 40/40, tonight is Thursday and you know what that means!

"All the sexy Corporate Chicks are hanging out!" they all said giving each other a pound.

"Alright, Alright, I feel you, true that!" Terrence said enthusiastically.

Dre followed suit. They went towards the double doors to exit, and headed in the direction of lounge.

As the fellas were walking Ant broke the silence "You dominated the conversation in the restaurant for about an hour solely talking about your poems again." The boys started laughing, but Ant said "I'm serious" "You got to limit us listening to your corny ass poems to once a week." "I get up with yall to bullshit, not feel like I'm still at work." "Approving this, Disapproving that" Granted that stuff may work on the ladies, but I get tired of hearing "I love you for this or how special you are, your poetry makes you sound more like a punk." "Dog, you not making me connect with my feminine side, you feel me?" So tone it down some when we all chilling together, because it's starting to be a bit much. I know Dre is not saying much right now but we spoke on this before. "Unless I'm putting my love inside, and I got a honey dripping wet for me, poetry is not all that useful." "It's not that serious, it's really not." Ant was still rambling on.

"You finished?" asked Terrence. "Your ass wasn't saying that about three weeks ago, when you told me give you a couple of lines to say to that honey you picked up at the 40/40" and didn't you "hit it" on the first night, because she was so taken by "your words?"

"That's true man" Dre jumped in.

"But you know what?" "It's all good." "We're still cool" Terrence increased the pace of his strides. "You don't want to hear it so frequently?" "Then dude if there is a next time when I ask you, just say no!" "Now let's get to the lounge to make it do what it do." Tonight should be another interesting evening, he thought. "Honies here I come."

3

You want to tell me who you think I am,
When nothing could be further from the truth,
As your "definition" of me
Lacks so many levels of accuracy,
I will let you know when,
If the day ever comes that you say something about me that
is true,
I suggest if you want to throw stones, then the person you
should look at,
Should definitely start with <u>YOU</u>!
I have done nothing wrong; I have not violated your trust,
Always have and always will be completely honest with
you,
Then what do you turn around and do?
Knock me down because you knew I was vulnerable.
Did you think because as a strong woman, I do not have
feelings?
Did you think that I would not be bothered by your
"harmless" dealings?
Initially, I thought you completely understood me,
Or at least had how I felt as your primary concern,
Well the harsh reality of it all is that wasn't the case,
Another tough lesson learned
In life we all make choices,
Part of staying positive and being happy,
Lies in the hand of whom? The individual…
And I know I am not the "ugly", "guilty" party in every
argument, every escalated disagreement you made me out
to be,

Honey if you wanted me to be there for you, then you
needed to be there for me.
All of your words, oh yes they hurt me, they cut like a
knife,
But I learned to deal with these things as they only make
you stronger in life.
So here we are today,
Yes I am fine,
A positive ray of light called "God's Sunshine"

       Tamika closed her notebook and smiled another
work of art complete. "Once my book takes off, Ain't no
Stopping me now, I got the Groove." "No Stopping, No
Stopping, they'll be No Stoppin!" singing into her pen. I
have extremely too much fun by myself, I hope this is
normal, talking and singing in cluttered spaces, laughing
and carrying on. Again, her phone interrupted. "Damn" I
have to take this call, if not she will blow up my line too.
She flicked open her cell, "Hey girl."

       "Hey" "What's up?" came through the receiver.
"You move to the Dumbo area of Brooklyn, and now you
don't know anybody all week," asked her friend Stacy.

       "Girl, must I remind you that I am grown, and yes
you said it correct I just moved so obviously I didn't have
time to be on the phone like that." Tamika was not fond of
the interrogation. "Ok, Stacy I know you didn't call to get
on me for *not* calling, so what's been up with you through
the week thus far?"

       "Nothing really" you know I am used to speaking to
you a couple times during the week, but since you asked
"Girl are you ready to go out tonight?" You know it's

Thursday, the weather is beautiful, and I know you have an abundance of hairpieces you can throw on your head to make yourself look fabulous. "So you down to get your social flirt on, or what?"

"I don't know girl", I am not really in a partying mood. I left work early, and I'm not even properly dressed anymore.

"I am not going to settle for that excuse about not being dressed" it will take you about a half hour tops to throw something on. Not to mention you know Jackie, Ann, and I know where you live, and are not afraid to roll up to your place, and drag you out. In addition, tonight I have something to celebrate that is all I am going to say. "So what's it going to be my way, or my way?" she asked waiting for a response.

"Girl you are truly crazy" "I will let you get that one making you think your threat is the deciding factor with me going, but in all honesty, it's really not"

"Well say what you want, I got my Yes." We are going to the 40/40 club; they are having some type of celebrity bash there so we get to rub elbows with the stars.

"So how much extra is it going to cost me to rub elbows with someone?"

"Nothing if we get there before 7:30 p.m."

"What time is it now girl?" Tamika wondered. "Ten after 6." "Ok, I will meet you, I will just be getting to the spot at 7:30, and if I have to pay so be it"

"Girl you know the bouncer at the door likes you, you're covered and we're rolling with you."

"Now you know it's whatever with dude, I'm not interested," said Tamika.

"See you soon; I am going to let you get dressed with the quickness."

"Sure, cut the conversation short now." Tamika laughed. "I'm not talking what you want to hear." "But if you want to date him you are more than welcome to."

"Bye girl."

"Ok, bye." It will be great to get out the house though, but please God do not let anything or anyone spoil the night. I don't need that right now. Fingers crossed.

4

"Yeah, so I'm saying you gon' come thru tonight or what?" "You know it's been a minute, and I want to see you". "Yeah...Yeah... I know I don't call all the time" "You know what? I don't have time to talk relationship with you right now, if you don't want to come over, don't, Good-Bye!" Terrence nearly broke his cell, slamming it closed the way he did. "Why do I bother with these broads?"

"You better not even say anything." Terrence said to Dre as he saw his lips about to part. He laughed because he answered that question as soon as it popped in his mind; of course it was for "some action." I am getting older, and I want to settle down, but shit tonight as if any other is not about "Mrs. Right" it's about "Mrs. Right now".

Dre spoke his mind anyway. "You don't want a woman right now and you know it", you have serious commitment issues.

"Dre, you know me but not on some deep level, so just chill". When I find the right one, she will not need or want anyone else. Terrence was all too sure of that.

"Damn!" With all this walking we still not there yet? Ant's face was pouring with sweat. He knew if he walked in the building looking all "funky" he wouldn't be noticed by many women. Ant needed to lose a couple of pounds, and it was times like this when it truly showed.

A few more blocks man, a few more blocks. "Stop Bitching" said Dre. "You acting like a lil' Bitch right now, acting all paranoid and shit, man they just smoked your cousin." They all burst out laughing in the middle of the street.

That line from "Menace to Society is classic." Dre, you are stupid for real!

Just then, the trio's joke became interrupted by Terrence's cell phone. "Hello" he replied.

"Terrence?" a soft voice inquired on the other end.

"Who else is it going to be, and what do you want?" "Actually look Kenya; before you say anything, I'm done." You want more, and I can't give that to you right now; so there's nothing more to say. "I am in the middle of chilling with my boys" but if you still have something you would like to say, then make it quick.

"Baby" all I wanted to say is, #1, don't hang up the phone on me again, or you and I...we'll have some serious problems and #2, is let me still come see you tonight, I'll take care of you, friendship with benefits; it's cool.

Okay, Okay, now you're talking! We definitely can link up. I should be home no later than 1am. "What made you change your mind?" "You know what?" I don't even need to know all of that. "Just take a cab over, and wear that sexy outfit I like."

"Alright babe, see you then" were the last words he heard her speak. Just like that the conversation was over, and Terrence had a devilish grin on his face. It is always so easy.

Terrence completely zoned out while walking with his boys. He found himself becoming aroused at the thought of Kenya coming over. Kenya was tall, slender, a very attractive young woman. She is 23 years of age and gullible, his type of conquest for the moment. Always pressing for a relationship but every time manages to find a reason to be able to deflect her from pursuing it. She stops by his place, he rocks her world then things are fine. She completely forgets what she should be getting out of their arrangement, not just tending to his needs. This has been routine for the last 3 ½ months. Snapping himself out of his daydream about later on tonight, he saw the Blue "40/40" sign flashing about a block away. He also saw a line that wrapped around the corner. Not worried about the line, he knew half the scrubby dudes wouldn't be able to get in anyway. They always hold shit up. Once they looked at the scuffed up shoes, or dingy armpits on the shirts of what the "Professionals" were wearing, he knew the only thing they would hear is "Access Denied". Then the real men could enter. This morning he paid special attention to wear attire that screamed "Ladies number one draft pick right here." Selecting his favorite designer, Salvatore Ferragamo, he completed the look with a Classic Fit- White Button Up, coordinating Black Slacks of the best Italian Material, and brand new Patent Leather Oxfords.

"Yo" this line is crazy as they walked towards the end of it.

"A celebrity bash, nice weather, and throw in the fact that it's pay day for some" you got a full house said Terrence.

"Don't sweat this line" chimed Dre, we're good. "Relax, that's why ya ass sweat so much, because you're always worrying." Ant didn't respond he just stood there unmoved.

5

"Keeping Sexy, Classy, and professional" in mind she peered through her closet. There wasn't much to choose from hanging there as many of her belongings were still boxed. A "BCBG" number jumped out at her; an all black collared v-neck shirtdress. "Black always makes a statement" it's not too short, and hugs all the right places. "I will whip out the peep-toe stilettos, and there I'm done." That took no time at all, great.

From the outside looking in, Tamika appeared to be a beautiful, high maintenance, fashion-savvy woman; however, she was not entirely, what people perceived her to be. She did not like spending a lot of time on creating her look, whether it was for a night on the town, or a day at Corporate America. Do not get it twisted though, Tamika knew she was beautiful, took pride in herself and her appearance, but wished men and women alike would look beyond that. There were many facets to this intelligent young woman. She longed for the day when the right man would peel away at all the layers, and get to what lies underneath. Her past was a tumultuous one, but with all that has happened, she still managed to look toward her future with optimism.

"Calgon take me away, is how I feel, but I don't have time for an evening of pampering if I am to be there by 7:30 pm."

"Therefore, in I go for a quick shower." Mika loved that she had one and a half bathrooms. The half bath was right outside in the hallway. The main bathroom was in her bedroom, talk about convenience!

"Time check" she turned her head to glance at the digital clock, "6:30pm" it displayed.

"My time management skills have gotten so much better" pleased by that, she entered the bathroom. She let the clothes she was wearing fall to the floor, and stood in all her nakedness. Mika turned on a small amount of cold water, and then began to turn on the hot water. The mix was a result of having the water as hot as she could naturally stand it on her body. The steam from the shower was like a facial to her. She stood there for a few moments, letting whatever stress she had go down the drain. She picked up her loofah, and Ocean breeze scented bath wash, and began to massage her body. Initially, she didn't have time for pampering, but she thought "Oh what the heck" if I get there a little past the meeting time so be it. She extended her arms, washing one after the other. Then she arrived at her breasts, she made sure to give them special attention. She made circular motions around her nipples, which were already hard. It had been quite some time since she had been satisfied, those reminders resurfaced at the oddest of times. She went on to cleanse her belly button, erotic garden, legs, and the rest of her sexy statuesque body. Feeling rather sensual, she gave herself a final rinse before she did something that only her, and her hand massager would understand. "The devil is a liar." "God help a sista…"

In between reaching for her towel, and calling out to cast away her sinful thoughts, her doorbell rang. "Who could that be? Dripping wet, she opened the bathroom door, and scurried down the hallway. She was mindful of her boxes so she would not trip or stub her toes. "Just a minute" she yelled approaching. Looking through the peephole before unlocking the door, she saw three magnified heads. She may have moved to a posh area of Brooklyn, but she knew it was still Brooklyn, and you still have to watch yourself.

"Will you open this dam door?" "I see your eye in the peephole." "We have been standing outside for five minutes," said none other than Stacy.

"Ok, hold up a second" Mika fiddled with the locks, but within a few clicks they were entering the apartment.

"Hey Ladies" you are sneaky! So you were already on your way when I spoke to you huh? Mika said after kissing the cheeks of Stacy, Jackie, and then Ann.

"I thought I told a certain someone to be ready in a hurry so that they could meet us on time." Stacy's voice echoed off as she entered and immediately began giving Mika's place the once over. She stopped just before reaching her bedroom. "Tamika Grace, you have a beautiful place from what I see, mess and all." The girls uniformly agree.

Mika bashfully said "thank you", as they all stood around their opinions deep down actually mattered to her.

Stacy, Jackie and Ann, together at the same time to hang out, that is amazing. Jackie and Ann came into the friendship pool later, when they were teenagers. They all went to the same High School, and can't be any more different. Ann has and always will be about having a man in her life, no matter how she is treated, suffering from a severe case of low-self esteem. Then you have Jackie who is, slightly older, college educated, yet her life is on cruise control every day. Always throwing caution to the wind. They all loved each other, but the older they became Stacy was sure those differences would divide them. Well divide Jackie and Ann from her and Mika she thought.

"As you can see, I don't have everything together, but I'll give you the full tour once I'm completely settled" Now, ok, quickly, we can move the party into my room, walk straight ahead. I mean we are going out tonight, right? So let's get it started!! Sit on my bed so yall don't mess up ya gorgeous outfits. "Look at my sistas, looking like the money making Divas you are!"

Jackie interrupted by saying "Compliments will get you everywhere."

"It'll get you a whole lot more if you had a long, hard piece of wood in between your legs too." Ann whispered to Mika as they shared a private laugh. Mika looked at her signaling to stop it.

"Alright I'll behave" Ann winked, as to say "yeah right."

"Excuse me", I need to reach over you to get my dress, grab my make-up bag and apply a few touches to complete my ensemble. Just going to step into the bathroom for a moment, "I have a small radio on my dresser, with a hot Dance Mix in there" put that on.

Ann took the initiative to play the CD. "Pop Champagne" was the first up.

"Damn is this as loud as it goes?"

"Um, what do you expect from a little boom box?" "Must you all always find something to complain about?" Mika seemed a little irritated. "Girl just go in my kitchen and bring the bottle of Red Alize, and cups" be careful so you don't hurt yourself in the mess.

"Girl, you know I'm just teasing right?" "Lighten up." off to the kitchen Ann went.

So let's catch up. I can still hear in the bathroom you know. "What's new with my girls?"

"Well you know Greg, I think he is cheating on me" said Ann whose voice was traveling down the hall.

"Ok, before you even continue, let me repeat myself." "I said what's new?" "Girl nothing for nothing your man is always cheating; and you know it and everybody in this room knows it, you stay so that's on you." Mika had a low tolerance to keep hearing Ann complain of the same situation for years now. Leave or stop talking about it was her motto.

Stacy cleared her throat to share her good news. "I just got promoted to Senior Accountant of my law firm, and in this economy that is unheard of." "I was saving my news for when we arrived at 40/40 but I couldn't wait any longer!"

That is wonderful girl, truly awesome!

"Yeah awesome" said Ann dryly, reentering the room.

"Oh stop hatin" said Jackie. When you stop making a man your priority, you will have some good news to share as well. As you will have what some of us like to call "A life." Can the church say Amen?

"Whatever" said Ann, "I know you are not talking" you're the female with the biggest man problems I know.

"Whatever! Back at ya" Jackie obviously up for the verbal battle. "Difference between you and I sweetheart, you're in a relationship going nowhere, and I am free as a bird." "I can make as many mistakes as I please and keep it moving" "You hate all the time!" "Damn girl do you get up and drink a glass for breakfast each morning?"

"Enough is enough! I love yall; but return to your respective corners please." "Check me out, Check me out." "I am ready to go!" Now I look good enough to roll with my girls. "But we're not going anywhere before we have our drink". Pouring the Alize in their cups, Mika raised hers after filling them to the brim and made a toast. "Here's to life and lasting friendships, if you can have longevity in both then you are truly blessed, and that's how I feel, Cheers." "Oh, and can't forget to say Congrats to my girl Stacy, staying on her corporate hustle."

"They smiled, tapped their cups and downed the Alize."

"Now I'm ready to get my dance on, to the club we go!" Mika grabbed her keys and clutch, as they headed out the bedroom. She clapped her hands together and the room went black.

"Did yall just see that"? This heifer has the clapper! "Oh my God" they couldn't believe it. They still make those? Um, someone please find Mika because she just transformed into an 80-year-old woman.

"Hey" don't knock it until you have tried it, and by the way ladies it's the improved Clapper2, now keep walking, keep walking. That made for a good laugh amongst the four.

She left the light on in the hall to give the appearance that someone was still home. They made their way out the door, as Mika locked up Jackie questioned, "Whose car are we driving?"

I mean is it really a question, said Ann "The BMW or the Jaguar"?

Mika made the choice simple for them "Let's give Stacy's car some shine; it's all about you and your car with your little animal to lead the way. To the elevator they went. "Why he gotta be a little animal is all I'm saying?"
"That's all I'm saying though."
"Stacy, chill out."
"I'm cool, sorry."
The elevator arrived…

A few seconds later you heard a "Ding, Dong"..
Here we are first floor everyone out.

6

Ring, Ring, Ring...Flicking open his cell phone, not recognizing the number, Terrence said "Yo, who is this?"

This is the promoter Jay down at the 40/40.

"Okay, what's up man? What can I do for you?" asked Terrence.

I know this is really last minute; however, we came across your name on our roster for our open mic line up, scheduled for this upcoming Wednesday. I am not sure if you're aware but tonight will be one of our biggest parties of the year.

"Yes I'm aware" Terrence answered, wishing he would get to the point. I am actually outside on line with my boys right now.

"That's perfect" said Jay. Listen, I don't know how you slipped thru the cracks for tonight but if you're up for it, you've got five minutes or less to recite a little "something, something". Tonight is our celebrity bash, and we promoted the open mic heavily underground so we would have only the best. We know you do your thing. Like I said, I don't know how you got past us, but if you perform and win by unanimous vote of the 3 celebrity judges, you could walk away with $10,000. "Are you in?"

Terrence was quiet, mainly because he felt slighted at the notion of being an after-thought; but $10,000 was at stake, and this is what he was born to do, so he replied "Hell yeah" count me in.

"Great" come to the front of the line, so we can get you situated. Showtime is at 9pm, you already know how this goes.

Stepping off line, Terrence signaled for his boys to follow him while he announced there's been a slight change of plans. "Good news is we're up off this line" the other news is this went from being a social outing to me handling my business. "I'm about to be paid!"

"What the hell are you talking about?" They asked.

"Listen" tonight inside is open mic starting in a little over an hour or so, with the winner walking away with 10k. You know that is the highest prize to this day, that I'm about claim right?

"My dude, say no more, let's roll." Ant did a sprint off the line.

Terrence busted out laughing, and said "Ha Haaa who is acting all supportive now?" "Remember your speech earlier?" Still amused, he managed to say let's get this paper.

7

Can I help you? Asked the bouncer that had this look on his face, as if you even think about starting something you will kiss the floor before you had a chance to realize what hit you.

"Hey man," name is Terrence, Terrence Jackson. We came to the front of the line because I should be on the list for tonight to perform. These two men, Anthony and D'Andre are with me.

Ok, step to the side to verify. Out comes a walkie-talkie like device. "Jay," come in.

"Yeah Scott" what can I do for you? Do we have a front door situation?

"No" I thought all the performers were in; just wanted to know are you expecting a Terrence tonight?

"Yes, Yes" forgot to tell you that, if he is there apologize for the inconvenience and let him through. This was a last minute addition to the roster.

"Okay, cool". You fellas can go right in; I have confirmed you on the list.

Now inside, Terrence peeked into the smoke filled room. His boys immediately went to the bar. The lounge nearly packed to capacity, never has it been this large of a turnout. Mentally he psyched himself up, how word must have traveled through the streets about how good he was. Realistically he knew it was the 90-degree weather and that it was a "pay-day" that convinced people to come and hang for a little after work relaxation. Terrence always found Thursday's at 40/40 interesting, where he has previously delivered his spoken word. Tonight there was much more riding on this, 10 Grand to be exact.

He proceeded to go to the backstage area. There was a certain aura of positivity floating about in the atmosphere, and he was drawing from it behind the scenes. His momentum building but was interrupted by the voice of a stocky young man. "Let's get ready for business people!" came from far left. It was Nephew Johnny accompanied by Steve Darcey of the "Steve Darcey Morning Show" on WBBS. They were the emcees for the evening, and wanted to be sure that everyone knew their order of appearance, before going out to entertain the crowd.

"You Sir, come here" Terrence looked around as to see if Johnny was addressing him. As he drew nearer, he questioned, "What is your name?" "Terrence."
"Terrence Jackson, just made the cut for this prize up for grabs huh?" Johnny looked up, smiled at him, and said you are last. We added you and downsized the list overall, there are only three artists scheduled to perform tonight. We may lose the crowd if we extend it beyond that. Everyone was given instruction on what was going to go down, where to enter the stage, and how many minutes he or she had for the set. All was completed backstage, and the evening was about to get underway soon. They instructed the performers if they had to step out to make a phone call, socialize, or whatever, to make sure they are

back inside by 8:55pm. If anyone were late, they forfeited their chance to participate.

8

The signs checked out we are safe here no street cleaning until 5am. "Parking found on a NYC street; unbelievable!" The girls were all excited. Even better than that, we are right in front of the club.

Can someone say VIP? Jackie jumped in to remind them that it is now 8pm, and who knows what crazy amount they are going to be charging now.

"Mika" Is that you?
Someone called out to her. She looked to the right and it was Scott the bouncer, at the car window scaring the hell out them. He was motioning he would like to open her car door, but first she needed to unlock it. She obliged. Stacy whispered to the girls as they got out the car, that man has eyes like a hawk, how did he see her on the passenger side? He is sweet on our girl, and could spot her a mile away, I bet you any amount of money. One thing is for sure we inherited her good fortune because we are not paying for anything tonight.

"Hey Scott" Mika replied as she flashed her million dollar smile at him. "I see a brotha is always working hard!" "What is up with the line tonight?"

"Don't you even worry your pretty little head over that, you and your girls can go right in." "I saw the nice Jag pulling up, and I was like who is that sexy woman in that car?" No offense ladies, but it was you. "You all want a table?" I got a few available.

"Sure, that would be nice; you know give the feet a rest before they start burning later when we're all dancing."

Scott just looked straight into Mika's eyes. He wanted her bad. She knew it, but he was not breaking her down. He simply was not her type. He made fruitless efforts, every time he saw her at 40/40. Nothing was too good for her. She always received complimentary bottles of whatever she wanted; VIP seating; or Comp admissions for her and a guest even if it happened to be another man. He wanted to show he could handle competition like a man. Now she took the benefits, but he was getting nothing in return except some conversation.

"When are you going to let me take you out?" he asked. She responded with the same answer as always "How about I get back to you on that?"

"Yeah, ok, cool" Just remember, I have a feeling one of these days you will say yes Tamika, I will be the one you need. "Yall go inside to the first table directly in front of the stage, enjoy your experience at the 40/40." He winked at her and said, "I gotta get back to regulating this line."

They entered to the sounds of Rell, "All this love". Jackie began to yell trying to talk over the music, asking the ladies what they would like to drink; she is going to the bar. Mika said well we already started drinking Alize at the house so we need to continue with that.
Let us go for, four "Thug Passions" a Hennessy and Alize mixture. They all glanced at each other and saw where Mika was headed in her thought process. Let's not worry about tomorrow; we are going to have a wonderful evening tonight!

Jackie said, "Thug Passions it is" anyone disagree? "No?" then cool. I will meet you all at the table.

Approaching where they were instructed to sit they pulled the chairs out from the table.
Ann said "Someone, if not all of us are going to be hung over tomorrow."

"I know isn't it great" said Stacy, with her fake smile plastered on her face.
"This is nice" from this angle we are able to observe everything, and everyone.

"Oh Look" Jackie is waving she needs help with the drinks. Damn that was fast we just sat down. Ann got up from the table and said, "I'll go help her."

"Cool, cause we're thirsty" Run along now. Stacy always managed to get under Ann's skin. Ann just rolled her eyes, and walked towards the bar.

Stace, before the girls get back let me holla at you, you need to stop this bickering with Ann. It's not conducive to continuing this friendship.

"Now girl you know." I am going to stop you right there. "This so-called friendship is holding on by a thread, we just tolerate one another." However why stop when it's so much fun? "Besides that child doesn't mind, she loves to play mental gymnastics with me, going toe to toe. Stop worrying, everything is cool. We are all grown we know what we can handle and what we can't.

"Excuse me, Excuse me!" My God, imagine what this place will be like in another 2 hours! Ann stop talking and just watch where you are going. Ann was trailing behind Jackie back to the table.

"Heyyyyyy" drinks are here. Jackie gave her best impression of her ghetto voice, as she placed two on the table. Ann placed the others down as well.

"Now" let us toast once again, before Mika could finish her thought, Stacy said "I got this one".

"We may not always see eye to eye, there may even be a period of time when we don't speak on a regular basis, but we all have love and respect for one another the way real sisters should." "I am glad to be here with you all tonight let's embrace the blessings that are going to come our way for the future." "Cheers." Now there I am done, yall lushes can down your drink.

"Come again?" said Jackie.
"Stacy", I'm about to stage an intervention for your social drinking. You want me to go get you another drink already right? Tell the truth. She joked trying to maintain a straight face.

Terrence decided he needed to see what was happening on the opposite side of the curtain. He couldn't get over the turnout tonight. There were people standing along the walls, that did not have a table reservation, and still there were more at the door trickling in. As his eyes traced the back of the room looking for familiar faces, he did not see any besides his boys. As he was about to release the curtain, he stood there in awe of her smile. There were four unfamiliar women sitting right beneath the stage, content with their drinks and having a great time; but she caught his attention. Flawless skin, caramel complexion, and no wedding ring on the left hand resting atop the table, He thought, "I will definitely holla at you later beautiful". You keep that smile going, and on that note, he let the curtain fall into its natural position, time to refocus, as it was almost Showtime.

9

The music dropped down a few decibels and the lights began to dim. The spotlight directed towards center stage. A man accompanied by a mature looking woman, with a gorgeous short Halle Berry haircut stepped out and asked: "How's everybody doing tonight?"

"Fine" the audience roared back.

Good evening everyone, I am Steve Darcey and this is my co-host Sheryl of the WBBS morning show. Nephew Johnny will join us shortly; he's running around here somewhere. Our other radio family member Carlita could not make it tonight.

"Are yall ready to have a good time?"

"Yeah"! The audience shouted.

"No, no, no" that was weak. That must have been the fellas cause my ladies came out to represent, Right? Sheryl said, as she stood adjacent to Steve as if she wanted to issue a Man/Woman challenge.

"Ladies", I said are yall ready to have a good time? In unison, the ladies gave a fervent "Hell Yeah"!! Now that's what I'm talking about.

"So what you think about that Steve?" as she strutted across the stage

Not to be outdone by the ladies Steve chanted "Do my Fellas run this mutha?"

"Hell Yeah"! they answered, then Fellas, "let the dogs out", and in that moment the dog pound was unleashed. The crowd was definitely ready to get the night underway.

Steve unofficially declaring himself the victor, turned serious for a moment. I'd like to take this time out to tell you what we have planned for you tonight. As you know we have some of the best-spoken word artists in the city here to share their material with you tonight.

"Woo-hoo, yes"! Mika yelled excited; her cheer broke through the silence administered by the attentive audience. The girls looked at each other smiling like their Hennessy/ Alize combination must be starting to kick in.

Steve acknowledged Mika saying well alright, "Woo-Hoo"! We have a fan of poetry in the house; I know at least one of these performers backstage must be happy to have front stage support.

Sheryl intervened to keep the upbeat pace of the evening; we also have several special guests in the house, let's give it up for Dwayne Wade of the Heat, La La and Carmelo Anthony of the Knicks, and hip hop sensation Drake. You never know who will be in the building! Ladies and gents please continue to show love by putting your hands together for Jaheim. Shortly, he will perform his hit single "Age ain't a factor"

Jaheim stepped out when the spotlight appeared on him, he waved, sporting a low Caesar haircut and wearing a oversized royal blue-button up, with some charcoal grey designer jeans. Ladies we've struck it big tonight, yes indeed. "Is it hot in here or what?" "Whew"! Let us continue, "Steve" back to you.

Ok, we will see you later on in the show; looking forward to that performance Jah. Steve asked now who's ready to win some WBBS prizes? The crowd applauded. He said, "I need the first person with a Hundred-dollar bill to come onstage". People scrambled through their wallets, and a very beautiful heavyset woman who resembled Mo'nique emerged through the crowd yelling "I got it, I got it"! No one dared to try and beat her to the stage, as she was about 198 pounds; seemed as though she was trying to get the last chicken wing at an all you can eat buffet. Steve checked the authenticity of the bill and declared her the winner.

First of all "what's your name sugar"?

She said "Michelle".

Michelle "where are you representing tonight"?

"Bk all the way baby, Brooklyn stand up".

" A-ight, A-ight" Sheryl gave BK love, "Brooklyn's in the building". We have two passes for you to go see Alicia Keys live at Madison Square Garden. Now you know these tickets can't be bought anywhere as this event has been sold out.

"I know, I know" I tried to get these tickets but waited too long to purchase them, and now I can go for free "I'm so happy".

Sheryl inquired, "Who is going to accompany you"?

"I gotta think about that one."

"Well you decide and enjoy", but before you go tell everyone who just hooked you up with the hottest tickets in town.

"WBBS! No Doubt"!

"Thank you Michelle", watch your step as you exit offstage. We will have another big prize to give away after Jaheim's performance.

On that note, "we are ready to get started". Coming to the stage we have our first performer originally from Chi-Town but now a certified hard core New Yorker give it up for "Mekei".

"Mekei ladies and gentleman", "C'mon give him a nice warm welcome".

From backstage, Johnny reminded him five minutes maximum, he gave him a pound and then stepped out to greet the crowd.

"So you're from the windy city?

"Yes Sir, I am"

So you just blew into town and stayed; never returned home huh?

"I guess you could say that Sir" a straightforward answer was all Mekei gave, he was beginning to panic, he played it cool though.

All the while Steve was being his comedic self.
"Well we're going to step off stage and let you do your thing." Tell us the name of the piece you are going to recite.

"It's entitled My Window." Steve gave a perplexed look on his face and said "I'm sure Sheryl and I will be back on this stage before your five minutes are up". "And that is from my gut". "Crazy Ass Title", who writes about a window? I don't want to be premature so, "Go head man, good luck"

"Hello everyone" (clears his throat)

"Hello" heard from the audience.

"My window",
I stare out through it but nothing captivates me,
Left wide open like my soul,
It's cold,
Like these streets, except it's my window
Out into space the thoughts go
Do yall feel me?
Some may be confused,
About how my window gives me the blues
Because all you think a window is,
You see it as nothing more than glass
Well you are wrong…
I don't want to be another brother complaining
About how in jail
I had no window
I was wrongly accused
My life is the Shawshank Redemption
Tim Robbins played out my views
MY WINDOW!!!
Let me bring my voice down an octave,
I see fear, as you see me,
Because now I have your attention,
You want to peer into my window
I tell people, do you know what it's like to be confined
A physical prisoner, and one detained in the mind?
My window was the escape,
My window was the truth,
My window led me away from abuse
I saw fields of freedom,
I saw my window as the path away from my circumstance
My window, no ledge….
My soul heard music but refused to dance
My window a refuge,
The longer I stared the clearer it became

These walls would forever remember my name,
MY WINDOW!!

      Two minutes had passed since Mekei stepped foot
on the stage and he was drowning. People were just not
feeling his material, the audience began talking; whereas
you could hardly hear him anymore.
      He decided to wrap it up and said, "I'm gonna turn
the mic back over to Steve, Thanks N-Y-C".
      The applause grew incredibly loud as to say thank
you for not subjecting us to further torture. Steve stepped
on the stage and said "yall are cruel". Somebody lied to me
though, they told me you all would experience the best,
now if that's one of the best; we are all in for one heck of a
night. I hope that you'll have mercy on the next performer.
But yall knew as soon as he said My Window; we were like
"aww hell no"!
      As Steve was onstage he was beckoned by Sheryl to
come to corner stage momentarily; he walked over, she
whispered in his ear that Felicia had bailed. She was up
next so therefore Terrence would be closing the spoken
word portion of the show. Steve nodded to show his
comprehension. Since they were one performer short Steve
decided to give away another prize. Sheryl went back stage
and joined Johnny to inform Terrence of the changes.

      "Who wants to win some tickets"? asked Steve.
      "I want Jay-Z tickets" one audience member yelled.
      "Sorry mama", you'll haveto keep it locked to the
station every day to win those.

      "However", I do have some tickets to the Tyler
Perry Stage play "Madea's: The Have's and The Have

Not's" at the Beacon theatre for this coming Friday if someone can show a unique tattoo.

Before he could say anything further a voice from below yelled "right here".

"Well, come on stage honey" It was Mika; a bit tipsy she got her bearings to stand up properly. She walked around the girls at the table to make her way to where Steve was waiting. As she climbed the short four step- staircase she was giddy that she was about to win a prize. She then extended her hand, and moved in slightly closer to Steve in her mind seductively displaying the Chinese symbol etched on her entire lower forearm.
"Trying to bribe a judge sweetie, won't make you win"! "Now what is this you are showing me and what is your name"?
"I am Legend", "I'm kidding, I'm kidding", the name is "Mika", and this symbol means "God's Wonderful Gift".

"Very nice" said Steve. Unique indeed because for all I know it could say Steve Darcey in Chinese.
"You would like that wouldn't you"? Mika said reversing the flirtation back. She glanced down at the table to see the girls laughing away as Steve didn't know Mika could hold her own with a charming man any day. He winked and said "here are your two free tickets", Ms. Gifted Mika. "Now sit yo' drunk ass down" I'm just kidding sweetheart, "Congratulations to you".
Now, a perplexing situation is about to unfold; I see you are with three of your girlfriends, so two of em' ain't going to be happy. Good luck with that one. "Hey," draw straws that may work. The crowd chuckled. "Alright," you can have a seat.

"Thank you Mr. Darcey", and then Mika stepped down and reclaimed her seat.

Our last and final performer you probably have seen at different venues throughout the Tri-State. You have seen him on BET's Comic view, Showtime at the Apollo, oh wait a second this isn't comedy, oops, "my bad"! Ha Haaa. Ok, yall coming to the stage this young brother simply goes by the name of Terrence, and that's all he wanted me to say about him, so without further ado here he is.

Terrence was always nervous before he went on stage. He was confident in the material he presented to the audience, however it was like a ritual that he would talk himself into frenzy before he entered his comfort zone, which was performing in front of whom he felt were his adoring fans. Terrence knew that spoken word at various nightclubs throughout the NYC area was the gateway to bigger opportunities that he had planned. Clear your mind T, he said to himself. You're about to go out there and do your thing like you do on any given night. As he waited those last few seconds behind the curtain he decided to change up his poem. He had an agenda tonight, an agenda different from the others. There was an attractive young woman that would be sitting right beneath him, and he was going to get their paths to cross tonight. He knew the importance of words, and how they can enhance, or deflate a situation in a matter of seconds. His name was heard through the curtains, and while the love was still being shown he emerged center stage. It's Do or Die time.

"Hello, Hello".
"How's everybody feeling"?

"Good I hope".

I see the drinks flowing. The way you guys just did my boy Mekei I may need a stiff one myself but you know I'm here to represent and give you what I have to give. It's good to see so many lovely people out here tonight and that's real. Why don't you give yourselves a hand! Tonight is going to be about the ladies. Fellas before you start with the sighs, hear me out, there may be a line or two you can use from me later. I am kidding however, some of you may have seen me perform elsewhere and know that I usually address political or social issues with my delivery; but tonight I want to let the women know how special they are. Now fellas how can you disagree with that? In addition, for the ladies, I know everyone here tonight or the majority of ladies are looking for romance! We need to bring it back to those days. The title of this piece is entitled "What I would like"

What I Would Like To Do Is Get To Know You

To get to know how you do-that thing you do- when you are doing what you did to me the way that you do
To get to know your what's, when's, where's, and why's-the reason your eyes smile at me and how to prevent those tears you cry
To get to know your aspirations your goals and dreams-to look into your past, learn your fears and what they all mean

What I Would Like Is To Be There For You

To be there for when life is unfair for no reason at all-to encourage you and pick you up if you should fall-to tell you yes when the world says no and to ask you for the answers to things I don't know-to be there even when I am far away- to be able to finish the sentences you begin to say-to be there to investigate this strange game of life and the mysteries of late- and do all we can in helping to determine our fate- to be there if and when you need me the most-to express how I feel when I'm holding you close.

What I Would Like To Do Is To Get Close To You

To get close to you; to get so close to you
To get so close to you that I feel your heart beating inside my chest-so close that I sense your emotions that I can feel your happiness-to get close enough that there are no differences in your perspiration and mine-as our juices mingle and mingle our bodies intertwine and we get closer with time- I'd like us to gasp as we inhale each other and slowly sigh-I'd like to caress your body, your heart, your soul, and bring tears of joy to your eyes-I'd like to lick them, kiss them, and drink them as I internalize all that is you- to take it there with you until you contract, extract, lay back and moan-to have no fear while there and have you make "there" your home-to get so close to you that I'm a part of you-to get so close to you is what I'd like to do-to converge on you and merge with you-to feel every ounce of my desire simply surge through you- if what you feel, feels true perhaps we can pursue more fun and what comes will be more than something or someone to do

What I Would Like To Do-What I Would Like To Do
I'd Really Like To Do –If It Can Be Done With You.

Peace.

Terrence took a step towards the microphone stand to put it back in its natural position. The mic now out of his possession, he waved and made his quick exit off the stage.

Tamika was the first to applaud, as she was impressed. The audience followed suit, and Steve, Sheryl and Nephew Johnny made their way back to the stage. They said "keep it going for Terrence".

"Wasn't he awesome ladies"?

"Yessssss"! They shouted.

Fellas you can't hate he did his thing; we all want a sensitive brother like that to come and blow our minds every now and again.

Steve I think we have a winner, but I don't want to be presumptuous in declaring tonight's "Champ". What is the consensus between yourself and Johnny?

I vote in favor of Terrence.

The two men huddled together as if they were discussing an important play on a football game during Superbowl.

Uncle and I have come to agreement on a very difficult decision; after all who could not understand the depth Mekei conveyed looking through his jail cell window, metaphorically for life's window. "Right"!

Then we have Terrence, a bit arrogant, but props are given where props are due, he was on point with his content. He hit home when he said we need to take it back to romance. That he did, and it flowed. Therefore, we ask that both men join us, one last time onstage.

"Kiki Shepherd", Johnny was clowning Sheryl, will you please hand this $10,000 check to Terrence?

"With Pleasure", Sheryl took the check from Johnny; and the exchange led to her placing 10 Grand in Terrence's palm. Let's thank Mekei for participating.

The crowd showed him appreciation for his efforts, and he then made his exit. Sheryl motioned to Terrence "the man of the hour", any closing remarks?

"Yes", I just want to thank my boys in the back, Ant and Dre, and I want to thank the lovely ladies of NY for their support, and the brotha's too. Remember get back to the romance.

That concludes the spoken word portion of our show, and what a fine note that ended on. Be sure to get your drink on, network, and don't leave because the party is just getting started. Still to come; Jaheim will bless the stage to perform his current smash single "Age ain't a factor". On that note, the stage became empty, and the D.J. cranked up Lupe Fiasco's "Out of my head" featuring Trey Songz to draw people to the dance floor.

10

"Terrence" someone called. It was Mekei.

"Hey Man"! Just wanted to come and tell you great job. You know one playa to another I think you had half the room of women wanting to come up out their panties. The other half probably wanted too as well but you know their man was next to them looking hard as if you had better not like this dude, you know?

"I feel you, I feel you". Pausing for a moment, Terrence said, Mekei, I get that sometimes, brothers get intimidated because we're not the most vocal creatures, and then you got a dude onstage romancing their woman with words. So they looking at me like what you trying to do? I just laugh to myself, write my material and say what I came to say. Give your woman alittle extra attention at home, you know something out of the ordinary and you won't have to worry about cats like me, or any other man for that matter. However, in retrospect, I had a good time; it's always a pleasure. Just a tip, and no disrespect tone down the material and you will do fine next time. Maybe take a different avenue than the one you chose tonight, and the next show you will bust it wide open. I will make good use of this money though, so in a way I have to thank you. Since you said it looked like the ladies were ready to come up out them thangs, I better go find the one I had my eye on that was sitting right beneath me, before someone else comes and scoops her up, off what I set up tonight.

"Right below the stage?" Mekei questioned.

"Oh" that's the table of the four well dressed, good-looking chicks. Yes, I saw them, one won a prize tonight

but I don't remember the name right now. Anyway good
luck with that playa; whichever one you choose. You
know they say "the more the merrier".

"A-ight man" you be cool too, they stepped in
towards one another gave each other a pound and kept it
moving.

11

"Nice Set"! "Great show", "Loved it"! That was all Terrence heard while walking through the crowd making his way to the bar to order a drink. He felt fortunate to have so many people tell him they enjoyed his work. His mind now off performing he just wanted to chill, and introduce himself to his mystery woman. He did wonder where his boys had disappeared to since the show was over. They should have been the first ones to come up to congratulate. Punk asses probably left, and didn't say. Finally, at the counter he waited to place his order. He just leaned on the counter, nodding his head to that new Jaheim joint; the DJ was doing a mix, spinning it now before it was sang live, to let people get familiar in case they hadn't heard it. The music was thumping loudly through the JBL speakers. When the server gave the signal as to what would he like; Terrence ordered a screwdriver made only with Ciroc; he wasn't trying to get sick off the cheap stuff. As he waited for the bartender to return with his drink, he clearly overheard a few men near him saying,

"Dude thinks he's some modern day Denzel or something to have the women falling all over him; but I'm not buying into this poetry shit".

He knew the comment was directed towards him because in order for him to hear them, they had to yell over the music. He thought was it worth addressing or not? "No", he decided not to be on some childish bullshit.

The bartender handed him his drink and said, "this one is on the house, although with $10,000 sugar, you can buy everyone in here a drink right"?

Terrence handed her a $5 bill for a tip. Her comment gave him the chills, as if he was a walking billboard for a set-up. Everyone knew he had just won a large sum of money, and times are hard but he just shook it off. As much as Terrence tried, to get his grown man drink on, the talking became louder with another one saying...

"Yeah, I don't like dudes that think that they're better than me just because they got alittle talent".

Terrence was sipping his drink when abruptly his shoulder was tugged on, causing him to spill it. Just as Terrence clenched his fist, and was about to "set it" laughing commenced. Eye to eye with the man directly in front of him he said...

"Yall are the dumbest Muther ... man you fill in the blanks" look what you made me do. You go out and can't find anything better to do but act a fool in the club.

"Yo' did you see the look on his face"? It was just straight up blank, he didn't know how to react. "Drink $10", "making Terrence lose his cool; priceless". Two of the three laughing were Anthony and Shawn, another friend from around the way.

"I told them it was juvenile man, but they thought it was a good joke to play" said Dre.

"Bitch ass" you always trying to suck up to Tee. So we played a joke, man ease up. It's all love Bruh! Congrats on that prize money, you did it baby, we're paid. Ant extended his hand first for a pound but he saw Terrence was still shaking his hands dry. Shawn made the situation worse by continuing the laughter. The bartender handed him a tissue and said this one's on the house too hun and shrugged her shoulders.

Terence mumbled a "Thank you".

C'mon man stop acting like that you know we clown you all the time about this poetry stuff.

Anthony motioned, "Bartender can we get a round of whatever he was having, and your name and number please?"

She winked and said the names Angela and your drinks will be ready in a minute. I'd be happy to give out my number to the right person, and unfortunately you're not him.

"Damn" you sure know how to shoot a brother down. You will be just fine baby, now let me get those drinks.

Shawn tried to make amends, and gave his congrats as well. It would have been good if the rest of the crew were here tonight; didn't even know you were performing; thought that was two weeks from now. The homies I asked to hang out couldn't because the wifey's had other plans for them. So here I am hanging solo, until I bumped into these two clowns at the bar.

Terrence started laughing and was like I can't compete with that. I'd choose a fine lady to hang out with over you guys any day. He gave Shawn a pound, and said "that's what's up" glad you were able to catch me up there.

Angela returned and said, "that'll be $40 boys".

Ant looked at Terrence "pay up".

"Dude you just ordered these drinks and now I'm supposed to pay for them"?

"You just won the jackpot, I know you didn't think I was gonna pay."

"It's a check not cash, dumbass, and I don't need to be up here coming out my pockets for no grown ass man who has money to drink."

Angela interrupted and said, "if there is a problem I can get security, but I know someone is going to pay me".

Dre, said "no problem at all beautiful", whipped out his Amex Black Card, handed it to her and turned back around to his boys to give a quick lecture.
"Yall don't pull this shit again", real talk "it's embarrassing". "Yall screaming about whose going to pay like a bunch of women".

Angela returned handed Dre his card, and a receipt with the charges. He put his John Hancock on the paper, tipped her and returned the top portion to her. "Thanks sweetie" she went on to serve the next customer.

I am about to leave you fools to keep each other company, and I'm going to handle my business. Now if I don't catch up with you guys by the time this wraps up in the a.m. I will see you around the way, or call yall tomorrow. "I'm ten thousand richer my peeps".
"A-ight man do you baby", Shawn gave a head nod, and Terrence stepped off.

12

"Who's ready to get this party started?" "I can't hear you"!!!!

Just throw ya hands in the air, and wave em' like you just don't care, and if you ready to rock with my boy Jaheim somebody say "Oh yeah"!

"Oh Yeah" the audience responded.

"Oh Yeah" the DJ said back.

Ladies and gentleman I want you to stay right where you are and put your hands together for the "Multi-Platnium Billboard King" Jaheim. The intro to his original smash hit "Just in case" started to play, and then the R&B superstar appeared on stage. The club was in full swing party mode. People already were singing the lyrics aloud, dancing, and Jaheim encouraged audience participation, extending the microphone out to the crowd. If you knew the lyrics he wanted you to sing along.

"This is my song girl". I am so glad yall asked me to come out tonight. "Listen," I am going to go to the bar and get one more drink. "Anybody want anything else? I'm buying. Going once, going twice?

"Na, we're good" the girls replied.

Mika got up from the table. "Just in case, I don't make it home tonight, let me make love to ya for the last time baby" "Excuse me". Slide to the side she mumbled. Tamika two-stepped it all the way to the bar. By the time she reached the counter she was slightly annoyed from all the men grabbing on her like she was the only woman in the room. Then again, she felt she was a hell of a chick. Tamika was smiling, and was just asked with a faint distinguished tone of sexiness,

"Would you allow me the pleasure to make you smile like that?"

Tamika looked to the left of her and said "What?"

The name is …"Terrence".

"Yes, I know" I just finished watching you not that long ago, Tamika cutting his two-minute intro short.

"Look gorgeous"; I was just at the bar, and as I was walking through the crowd, I saw you. You don't know how hard of a task it was to get back here again, just to talk to you. You look like you can smell game a mile away, so I am not going to give you any tonight. It's loud in here, and this is not a proper setting to get to know someone. Unbelievably, I had my eye on you all evening. "You are breathtaking".

The bartender interrupted purposely. "What can I get for you sugar?"

"I will have a Henny and coke, thanks".

So as I was saying what a brother gotta do to get to know you better?

"Well", just as Mika was about to speak, her drink was placed in front of her.

"There is your drink sugar". That will be $13.

Terrence had to speak before they proceeded any further. "You're doing this on purpose right"? "Blocking"? Simply, because of what happened earlier with the tab? I like you Angela, you take real good care of me the previous times I've performed here, however you don't have to look out for her, I'm not a jerk just a couple of my friends. Here is $20 for her drink, keep the change.

"Alright Terrence" thanks. Be a gentleman is all I'm saying, and she walked away to serve the next customer.

"Wow" "Ok", that was weird, said Mika. "You two were intimate before?"

With a raised eyebrow, he asked her, "Now why would you say something like that"?

"I mean, it is just that a woman that does not know the other won't usually take that defensive position, meaning looking out". I guess life is full of surprises. And, speaking of surprises as crowded as it is, I am amazed at how fast she fixed my drink, so without any delay, down the hatch she goes. "Thank you" for the drink. I should be getting back to the table with my girls, not to mention I am missing Jaheim!!

"Oh no you don't sweetie". Terrence slid right in front of her before she had the opportunity to move any further.

"So you are one of those guys that buy a girl a drink and think I have to be with you all night?" I don't think so, if that's the case you can have your drink back, well the half that's left in the glass anyway. "Oh what do you know?" Looking at the glass, it's all gone. They both laughed.

"You have a sense of humor" I like that.

A round of applause ensued that further drowned the two out. Jaheim had just finished a song, and was about to start another, so Terrence took this as the opportunity to ask, "Mystery lady" can I have your name and number please?

"If I give it to you can and will you move out of my way?" Jaheim is looking for me!

"Ok, ok," agreed. I see you really like Jaheim, I am feeling slightly jealous, not in a crazy type way, but in a damaged male ego type of way. I mean what does he have that I don't?

"Boy, Please"!! Don't make me answer that. Terrence, my name is Tamika; if we become friends, you can call me Mika, since that's what all my friends call me. If we don't become friends you won't call me anything, she smirked. Now "Do you have a pen?"

"Yes, I do," liking her assertiveness.

"May I have it?"

"Yes, you may", he obliged eagerly to that request. He reached in his shirt pocket and pulled out a black ink pen.
"Thank you" said Mika. Extend your hand please.
"Huh?" said Terrence.
She said "hand".
He extended his hand towards her, she flipped it over so that his palm was exposed, and scribed 718-555-3470. Forget pulling out your cell phone we are going to

do this the old fashion way. Looking forward to hearing from you and with that she returned his pen, said pardon, and left him standing there in a fog. He felt like a star had just given her autograph. In that moment Terrence fell in "like". He thought she was definitely on his level, the stimulating challenge he hadn't come across in a woman in a long time. Ms. Mika, you have made my night.

"Girl what took you so long?" Thought you got kidnapped.

"Shhh"! Rock to Jaheim. I can answer all you heifers' questions after my future husband finishes serenading me.

"Could it be the ice you see? But you tell me that you're really feeling me? Could it be the word on the block? I know they told you that I got it on lock".

"Sing it Ja"! Mika had no shame in showing her appreciation of his music. He could sing about some odd topic and would not care. The girls knew when she was in her zone just let her be.

Jaheim walked through the crowd as he sang, passing out long stemmed roses to the ladies, but that didn't last very long as security had to intervene. The women tore at his clothes, reaching for his private parts, and became unruly. Security escorted him back to the stage, therefore "Could it be" turned out to be his last song of the night. Jaheim belted out the ending of his song A cappella, so you could recognize the sultriness that lied within his vocals. Jaheim gave a performance noteworthy of an Awards show. With that he thanked his fans, told them to go purchase his new album if they haven't already done so, and check his website for upcoming tour dates. The DJ went back to spinning tunes; the dance floor flooded with men who were glad to come off the sidelines while the women finished swooning over Jaheim.

13

"Well that turned out to be quite an experience women tearing at the man's clothes". That's why I am an average fan at best, not a groupie. That was ridiculous, because they didn't think that acting out of order, no one gets to hear any more Jaheim live. I did have a good night with you all. Glad I came out, we toasted our accomplishments, and it was fun.

Y'all had asked what had taken so long at the bar. "Well" there was a certain individual that performed tonight- Terrence, that I gave my name and number to. We will see if amounts to anything. It probably won't but he is kind of cute, Mika mused.

"So the window of opportunity for love has opened back up huh"?
Stacy waited on an answer.

"Girl, you think because I gave my number out that I can foresee where this is going to go?" Maybe just some telephone conversation.

"Why am I even answering you in the first place?" You are making me put too much thought into giving out my digits.

"So are we going to hit the dance floor, or are we calling it a night?"

"I say we party until the wheels fall off"

"Not a bad idea" they all agreed. The women gathered their purses, and decided to hang around until the club closed at 2a.m. The party continued.

14

My boys have gone home. I got this money. I am the man; no one can top the shit I do, the work I put in!

Now to cap my evening, I will get some loving from Tamika, well at least in my mind that's who I will be thinking of when I have sex with Kenya tonight, and she will be none the wiser.

Terrence exited 40/40 satisfied with the night's results.

He extended his hand to hail a cab to take him home. Kenya should be on her way shortly.

"I know how this is going to go" I will be standing out here for an hour, black man trying to flag a cab in New York City, they all afraid they going to get robbed. Dam shame.

A cab finally pulled over after 10 minutes.

"Man, am I glad you stopped".

"Where to Sir?" The driver was not concerned with making small talk.

"200 Empire Blvd" corner of Bedford Avenue. Terrence said scooting over to the center of the back seat. He glanced at his watch as it was around 12:15 a.m.

The metered cab was running but traffic seemed to be smooth from what he could see ahead, so the fare shouldn't be outrageous.

He liked the driver's style because instead of trying to "milk the fare", he proceeded through the yellow lights instead of slowing down, keeping a consistent pace. He would in Brooklyn in no time.

"Oh shit" Terrence looked in his palm. He was so proud of the fact he scored Tamika's number tonight he forgot to transfer the number in his cell. He looked to his palm and the number was still legible. He took out his phone and entered her name and number.

Just to verify that he had the right number he decided to send her a text, and see if she would respond.

"Hey Mika, calling you that because I figure we are already friends from our brief encounter (smile), you are truly something special, hope you and your girls enjoy the rest of your night, talk soon-Terrence.

<Send>

Then he glanced out the window to see they were in lower Manhattan about to cross the Brooklyn Bridge.

"Eh, man, can you take Flatbush Avenue straight once you enter into Brooklyn?" Then take whatever side street you wish once you get closer.

The driver replied "Yes".

A chime came through on the phone, indicating a text. OMW, meaning "on my way", it was Kenya.

Terrence returned to look out the window, cruising past all the parked cars on the crowded Brooklyn streets. He never sweats a woman, and if Tamika doesn't respond, screw her. I'm Terrence J; forget so much thought to a pretty face. She had better respond though, he told himself one time for good measure.

The driver continuing slightly above the speed limit, obviously wanting to get his passenger to his destination in a hurry; soon pulled up in front of his home.

The cab came to a halt, the meter reading $29.75.

"Guess it must be that night time differential huh? I figured no traffic, it would have been around $10 cheaper, but here you go my man $35, keep the change. He opened the door and exited the cab.

Terrence thought he was making it easier on himself, or the next brotha that needs a cab, showing the driver of Indian decent, that not all Black men are criminals to fear. He may have bridged a cultural gap, one dollar at a time. Probably not, but it was a worth a try.

Keys handy, he walked towards his Brownstone, walked up the steps, unlocked the doors, and proceeded to enter.

He turned the lights on, headed straight into his bedroom to strip down to his Joe Boxers, six pack on display, and placed his dirty clothes in a bag that will go to the cleaners in the morning. Looking around his room, it's as neat as it needs to be, he plucked the covers back, and made sure the sheets were clean, since he had another conquest over a few days prior and it was not Kenya. Yea he was ready for her, wasn't putting that much effort into a chick he digs out every now and again.

15

"Ladies my feet are looking like some sausage links right now". Jackie said.

"I agree" chimed Tamika.

Let's call it a night, I know we like to think we can still party like it's 1999 but those days are long gone.

Since the car is right outside, "Thank the Lord," we don't have to wait for anyone to go get it, we can hobble together.

Stacy asked "Everyone has everything right?

"Yes" we are all good to go, so towards the exit they limped. Tipsy, with hurt feet from heels and dancing they couldn't get to the car quick enough.

Scott was standing at the door and said "You ladies make sure you drive home safe"

"Do you all need me to call you a cab or anything?

"No, Scott" we can make it, we just have a little residual alcohol going on, but I stopped drinking over an hour ago so I am the designated driver. No drinking and driving for us; you are looking at some responsible ladies.

"Now are we free to go father?"

"No need to be sarcastic, I was just looking out"

"We appreciate that and I was just kidding with you."

"No hard feelings and see you next time."

"Have a good night"

Scott replied have a good night too. He didn't try to rap to Tamika upon leaving because he knew he wouldn't get anywhere with her friends running interference. They walked towards the car, disarmed the alarm, and opened the doors to get in. Just like that, they were all strapped in and you saw the car backing up, so they can pull out and be on their way home.

Tamika did wave to Scott to be polite as they pulled off she knew he was watching. He waved back.

"Why do you intend on giving that man mixed signals?" There went Jackie with her line of questioning again.

"It's funny how you can ask me that but when we were all getting something out of the deal it was ok to accept a complimentary table earlier?" I mean where was the question then?

"Ok, you have a point" Sorry.

"But to set the record straight, I don't like using people." Yes, we accepted the table the least I could do was say thank you, which I didn't before we left, so the next best thing to do was acknowledge that I knew he was there, and gesture; like see you next time. That was it. He probably would take it to mean more, but he knows how I feel and where I stand.

"Are we on the same wavelength now?"

"My, someone is defensive."

"I second that." Ann was now a part of this conversation.

Tamika didn't say anything else for the moment, she fumbled around in her bag for her cell phone. She pulled it out, and went to review any missed calls she received or text messages. She only received one missed call from a co-worker, which at this time of night she knew a return call would not come before noon tomorrow. Then she went on to review her messages, and smiled just a tad.

"I received a text from Terrence" she stated.

"Girl what did it say?" asked Stacy.

"Actually he said he hopes we all had a good time, and he called me Mika, like he knows me." That boy has some nerve, but he did make me smile though. I see he wants to make sure he leaves his name on my brain tonight.

"Well are you going to text him back?"

"I suppose so." I have to think about what I want to say though. Nothing too deep.

She simply wrote, Good morning Mr. Terrence, since it is after midnight. I appreciate the text, tonight was awesome, your spoken word was ok, and my girls and I had a great time, thanks for the text. <Send>

Tamika was reading the message aloud as she typed, and Stacy said "you crushed the man's ego telling him his poem was ok."

"Perhaps" said Tamika.

"How much are you willing to bet that it will garner another reply?"

"And just how do you know that?" Do tell said the group.

"I know this because like you said, I went for his ego. He is feeling me, not to be conceited but that's obvious in his approach to me at the bar. So with that he is going to want me to stroke his ego, since he thinks so highly of himself, and the more I don't, the more he is going to be interested. You know men like what they feel they can't have. It's just another form of the cat and mouse game played by people that are in the beginning stages of trying to get to know one another. You know I am not for the games, but once you filter through all the B.S. upfront then I can see who Mr. Terrence really is.

"Now who is putting all this thought into a relationship or taking it further?" Stacy said. When I asked earlier was the window of opportunity opening for love you shut me down quick, and now look at you! Girl I know you too well. You are interested you just trying to be hard-core. It's ok to show a vulnerable side to a man, not everyone is going to hurt you like...

"Stop right there" Tamika's voice escalated. Don't say his name; don't mention anything about that last jerk I dated. Just keep driving, my bed is calling me, and I don't want the evening to have an ugly downturn so let's just listen to the radio or talk about something else.

Tamika looked in the back of the car, and the other two had passed out. That didn't take long at all. I told you we can't drink like that no more. One minute you are up, then the next minute passed out and don't even feel it coming.

"Good luck" dropping those two off should they wake back up before you get them home, I feel your pain, but am not envious of your position. I am the first stop baby and happy about that!

16

Kenya had already arrived at Terrence's place. She aimed to please so she showed up on his doorstep wearing a short knee-length sweater type jacket, push-up bra, matching boy short, garter belt and lace stockings. There was a similar number that Kenya had wore previously that Terrence admired. She liked the fact that he ravished her that evening. She thought she had him right where she wanted him, but she like many others confused his lust for love. She too remained optimistic, that one day he would tell her she was the one. He opened up for her, when she let him know she was outside and immediately he kissed her at the door, and tugged away at that sweater to get it off. They barely made it to the bedroom.

Terrence had Kenya on her stomach, with her back arched and her "assets" up in the air. He pulled on her long brown shoulder-length hair with one hand, and the other around her waist pulling her closer to him with every stroke. She screamed and moaned loud enough for the neighbors to awaken, and that made him pound her even harder. They continued their session for another 20 minutes until the both reached their orgasmic climax, and then it was over.

Terrence did not cuddle Kenya, he rolled over to the far edge of the bed, as he did not want any intimacy with her. She tried to lean in towards him, but he just pushed her off.

She rolled over and saw something light up in the dark. The phone was on silent but it was ringing. It was an incoming call but no name attached when she glanced over. She took the phone and tossed it at him, and asked are you going to get that?

He looked at her took the phone, and simply replied "No".

He said "Now either you can stay here and go to sleep" or "you can gather your little belongings" and I will call a cab for you to go home.

Kenya, thought about it for a moment, and decided to leave. She had felt cheapened and used but it was her own fault. She knew how Terrence was with her, and what he represented. She still had hope that she could change him.

"Terrence just because you don't have a name tied to the number, don't think for a moment that I don't know that it's another woman calling you at this hour"

"I'm tired of being hurt by you."

"Why do you do this?"

"Am I not good enough for you?"

Terrence just wanted to get some sleep at this point. He picked up his cell, and began dialing; 718-555-0982.

"Good Morning"

"Yes, Liberty Cab can you send a taxi to 200 Empire Blvd?"

"How long?" Two minutes? Great.

"Your cab is on its way"

Reaching in his pants pocket, he said…

"Here is $20 for your fare." You don't live that far so it shouldn't be any more than $12.

"When he honks you can run outside, and make sure you text me to let me know you made it home safe." Thanks for tonight it was good seeing you.

"You are a piece of work Terrence."

"I hate you, yet love you so much."

"Everybody needs somebody, and you act like you have no feelings at all." I just don't understand.

"And maybe you never will, you are still young Kenya" You have time to grow and fall in love with someone else. Unfortunately, that's not what we have baby. You know this, but you refuse to wrap your pretty little head around that concept.

"Honk, Honk"

"There goes your cab" Terrence ushering her out. Kenya barely had time to tie the belt around her sweater jacket.

He walks her to the door, so that he can lock it.

She turns around and looks at him before leaving, indicating say something to let me know you care.

He says "Your cab will leave you better go."

She kisses him softly on his cheek, and says good-bye Terrence. I wish you well.

In her mind, she doesn't think she can do this anymore, so in case this is the last time she sees him, she wanted to end it amicably. She has to will herself not to call, or run when he comes calling, but she turned around, walked down the steps and entered the cab.

Before they even pulled off, Terrence had retired back to bed.

17

The sun gleamed through the window blinds, and awakened Tamika earlier than expected, since she had the day off she wanted to sleep in late.

She rolled over, got up, and made her way to the bathroom to relieve herself. A quick tinkle, wipe and flush and she was back sitting on her bed.

She then picked up her cell from the dresser, no messages or calls since she last checked.

Slightly disappointed, as she secretly wanted a reply from Terrence; she put the phone down, and decided to try and fall back asleep for a bit.

After all it was only 6 a.m. She pulled the covers over her head.

18

"Beep, Beep, Beep, Beep" Dam time to get up already? Terrence slammed the snooze button so he could sleep for another ten minutes. It was 7:15a.m.

"Beep, Beep, Beep, Beep" whoever came up with the snooze button needs to be told how dumb the concept is. Those few extra minutes of sleep you hope for are a waste of time. Better to get up when it first goes off.

Another day another hustle, to conquer. Terrence gave a big stretch before moving from bed. He thought about it for a second and decided, I just won a large sum of money last night, I can afford to take a day off from work. He picked up the phone and called his boss. His boss answered, and he said he would not be able to make it in today, he apologizes for the short notice, but there was something personal that he had to take care of. His boss did not go into detail over the phone; he just asked would he be in Monday. Terrence replied yes, and his boss said ok, hope he resolves what needs to be done and he would see him next week.

Both parties hung up the phone.

Terrence then began checking his phone messages, and his face lit up when he saw a text from Tamika. He was glad that he hadn't come across it earlier this morning because he probably would have responded, and he did want to appear overly eager to this woman he knew nothing about.

After reading the message he responded, "Good Morning Sunshine". Thinking of you, wishing I were in your presence to see your beautiful face. <Send>

19

Terrence put the phone down and decided to get showered.
He would make the most of today. Go get some breakfast
and go to the bank to deposit his ten thousand dollars.
Every time he thought of it he felt so accomplished, he was
heading towards the next level.

He headed in the bathroom, stopped at the sink, looking in
the mirror, and saw he could use a line up at the barbershop
too. Today was appearing to be another nice day so he
didn't want to add too much on his plate because he could
come back home and chill to work on some new material.

He turned the shower on, waited a few seconds for the
water to heat up, and then stepped inside.

He pulled the sliding glass door closed, grabbed his
washcloth and soap, and began to lather up.

Her vision will not fade from my mind,
Her elegance, Her class one of a kind,
I could be presumptuous in thinking this woman is for me,
I am willing to go beyond what the eyes can see,
It took me a long time to seek her,
Infatuated with this woman named Tamika

Terrence cut the water off, was clean as a whistle, and
exited the shower.

He grabbed his towel, wiped off some of the water and
wrapped the towel around his waist.

Entering his bedroom, he checked his phone, this time only receiving a text from Dre. Dre informed him of the weirdest thing; he said everyone heard he had won the prize last night. That part wasn't bothersome to Terrence at all, but the remaining part of the message was. He said some were happy, but some of the dudes from in the area feel like he didn't deserve it so he just said be careful if you suddenly find some people trying to be overly friendly. Terrence didn't like it but he said a Hater is always going to find a way to hate. Let the chips fall where they may, I got something for anybody who wants to come test me. He was referring to some ammunition, but he was just magnifying the situation in his head. Terrence had guns, but he was no thug. It was all talk.

He went to his closet, looking for something casual to wear for the day. He decided upon his Blue Kangol, light grey button-up, and some Blue denim jeans. He would top it off with a pair of J's. Can't go wrong with some Jordan's.

20

Tamika had awakened from her extended morning nap, and was washing the dishes as she had just finished eating breakfast, two hard-boiled eggs, turkey sausage, and a nice tall cup of French vanilla coffee.

She went back into the bedroom, checked her phone and saw a text from Terrence. It made her smile, it did. She had her reservations getting back into the dating scene entirely because men seemed to be so trifling, well some of the ones from her past; but that didn't mean she should dismiss them all.

"Good Morning Terrence, I know I'm alittle late in my reply, just seeing your message" <Send>

Hope you have a great day, make every moment count <Send>

"Ughhh" that last part sounded so cheesy. I hate texting sometimes.

Her phone beeped indicating another message received.

I would like to make my moments count with you. Let me take you out to a movie or dinner. Actually, whatever you want to do is fine with me. I just want to get to know you better. I am off today therefore you can call me if you'd like later. <Send>

What a coincidence, I am off today too. I just moved so I am organizing my apartment. If you are spontaneous, we can meet today, I have other upcoming scheduled days off so I can always finish what I need to do then. <Send>

Would you like to do a late lunch? <Send>

Terrence replied, "If you don't think it's too creepy, you can give me your address and I will come and pick you up around 12:30pm. Going to try to spend as much time as I can with you today, in case after we meet you decide you don't want to see me again. <Send>

I have a few errands to run and if you don't mind you can accompany me <Send>

"Sounds good." You had better not be a serial killer because I am calling my girls and they will have a thorough description of you in case something happens, and that's real talk. You can meet me near my house; Do you know where Luke's Bar & Grille is located in Dumbo? <Send>

Yes I do replied Terrence. <Send>

Meet me there at 1pm <Send>

Ok, see you then Ms. Tamika <Send>

21

Equally excited; Terrence and Tamika for their first encounter since the club last night, placed a lot of effort and thought going into their meeting. For Terrence it was more about finally getting to know someone on a deeper level, he didn't know what it was that had him so taken when he first laid eyes upon her. For Tamika, she had refused so many dates for many months now, she thought his approach was a bit different then other men so why not give him a chance. It didn't hurt that he had a love of poetry, and he was pretty good at it. That, was a common denominator to something of interest that they shared off the top.

Tamika phoned Stacy at work quickly to give the very few details she knew of Terrence if something went awry on their date.

"Ring..Ring…"

"Hello"?

"Good Morning girl", it's ya favorite bestie in the world, Tamika.

"Good Morning as well" I think I know your voice by now. Called to rub in my face that you are off today? You know a sista had 3 cup of Joes, and I am still not functional! It was totally worth it though, so what's up?

I was just calling to tell you, I am going out on a date.

"A date"? Tamika that is great you need to get out, and share some male interaction, but just don't give it up on the first date. As long as you've been holding out, I know you must be ready to attack somebody, Stacy laughed.

"This may not be a date." I don't know what to call it. I just called to tell you, I am meeting the guy from last night, Terrence. We are going to meet by Luke's, where we all go to hang out. I didn't get his license plate number, but we should be staying local in Brooklyn. I will text that to you when I get it. The only thing I remember from last night is he is tall. Nearly six feet, he is muscular, dresses nicely, has these dark brown eyes, his hair cut low, and so is his facial hair. He looked good last night when he approached me. I just wanted to give you a quick buzz to let you know what I was doing today. When I get a chance I will call or text later, you have a good day in between.

"You do the same girl." Can't wait to hear the details later. I'm going to get back to work. Catch ya later. And with that both ladies hung up.

22

By this time, morning had ended and the afternoon had approached. Tamika had begun walking to the bar where Terrence was going to meet her. He told her to look out for a Red Mustang convertible, he informed her he had two vehicles but since it was so nice out he figured they could let the top down, if she didn't mind the wind blowing through her hair.

Tamika said that was fine. She had her hair pulled back in a ponytail wrapped in a bun, and wore some gladiator sandals, and a strapless sweetheart dress, black of course, a color you're almost always sure to find her in.

No car in site meaning she was the first to arrive, as the bar was not far from her home. She went inside, the temperature was favorable, and so she decided to order a quick drink. Now seated, the bartender said "what can I get you?" She replied "A Sprite please". First, she wanted a cocktail but decided to hold off on the drinks until they met. Not having her complete wits about her for an initial meeting may not be sensible.

There was plenty of room to be seated within the establishment, but a man stood behind her and said I will have what she's having. Tamika turned around in her swivel chair, and asked how did you find me? "You are a stalker" admit it. You have the signs written all over you. They laughed. He said "No, not at all Ms. Lady". When I turned the corner, there were a few cars in front of me but I saw you, and those sexy legs up ahead entering the bar/grille.

"I'm glad I didn't have you waiting long"

"No you didn't" But I will say you only had a grace period of about ten minutes to be tardy and then after that I was leaving. It is good to see that you know how to be punctual.

"Are you always this straightforward?" Terrence inquired.

"Yes, I am" is there a problem with knowing where you stand with someone.

"Not at all Ms. Firecracker, I mean Tamika."

They again shared a laugh, and Terrence sat beside her as he no longer needed to stand.

Tamika, I have to tell you and I'm sure you hear this all the time. You are beautiful. I hope the outside matches the inside, but I am glad you responded to my text, and we were able to meet up today.

"Yea, yea, yea, Mr. Smooth" let me get a formality out of the way right now.

"Are you single, married, dating casually, in a serious relationship, live with your mama, have a baby mama?"

"Woah, woah, there!" Would you like me to leave and reenter so we can try this again?

Just then Mary J. Blige's Share my world came on the radio.

"See take this as a sign, beautiful day, and the atmosphere just slowed down about ten notches with the smooth afternoon tunes."

"It's going to be alright Tamika, I'm only here to get to know you and see what happens"

To answer your questions though, "No, I am not married, I don't have kids, I am not in a relationship, and I am dating casually." I mean if you haven't noticed, I am out with you right now, and you have my full attention. I am glad to be here.

Terrence silenced Tamika. She paused for a second, as if she was absorbing all that he just said.

"I apologize." I completely went over the top just now. It's just that I am not for all the games, if we're out and a female giving me nasty looks because that's your sidepiece, or your wife runs up on us right now because you should be at work, and you are out playing hooky, it would be a problem. I just want to know who or what I am dealing with.

"And that's fair enough" You attacked me the way you asked, but I respect that.

I will be more than happy to let you know more about me, but for right now tell me about yourself and don't hold back on the juicy stuff. Terrence sat very attentive awaiting her to start anywhere she wished.

"Juicy stuff huh?" You are funny.

Well, as I mentioned to you earlier, I just moved into my condo. That was a big accomplishment, because prior to that I had a roommate, and apartment living just wasn't for me anymore. It is a one bedroom, and a mess but in the next few weeks, it will look great. I will jump off topic for a moment and tell you we have something in common though. I write as well.

"Do you?" he inquired.

"Yes, I write poetry and songs."

"I wouldn't have been able to tell since you said my work was just ok in text."

Tamika laughed. She said "Oh that" I was teasing. I liked your whole delivery last night.

"Perhaps you can recite some to me when you feel comfortable, Ms. Lady."

"Are you implying I am shy?" Terrence, I am not shy about what I have confidence in. This is not something that I just picked up, I have been writing for a very, very long time.

"Go head girl" Exuding confidence, I am falling in love right now.

"Boy cut it out" and she smacked him on the hand playfully.

The chemistry between the two was undeniable.

"Ok, here is a little something for you."

I ran away from love when it knocked on my door,
Because if I let it in and it didn't remain,
I wouldn't be content yearning for more,
Why put myself through the turmoil, and the hurt so many cry about,
Love is something I can do without,
It may be a contradiction,
Because I feel love will find its way to me sooner or later,
And if it creeps up on me, the feelings may be even greater,
Than my heart can hold, more than my heart can stand,
I just hope that when love does arrive it will be for the right man.

"Tamika that was really good." It was short but filled with raw emotion, and I can tell you've been hurt really bad. The fact that you chose that one, out of all the material you say you have is a warning to me, and I hear you.

"No warning Terrence, that came to mind, so I recited it"

Listen, I have an errand to run, do you mind if we get out of here, we can return later if you want, or go somewhere else if the day continues to flow.

"I told you earlier, that's fine" so I am ready to roll.

With that, Terrence got up first, and then held Tamika's chair so it wouldn't move while she got up.

Terrence put a $20 on the table for the two sodas, and he extended his arm, as for her to walk towards the exit and he would follow.

She stopped short once she reached the exit because she was not sure which direction to walk.

"I'm parked on this side of the street at the end of the block"

"I see your car now, right in front of the stop light"

"Yes that's it"

The two walked and didn't say much else to one another for a few moments.

Once they arrived at the car Terrence placed his key in the passenger side door to unlock it, and opened the door for Tamika.

She liked the gentleman like behavior he exhibited.

He then walked around to the other side, unlocked his door, and got in the vehicle.

"So where are we going?"

"I need to go to a bank downtown so I can deposit a check"

"Oh, you mean THEE check from last night"

"Yea" that would be the one he replied.

"I could have had other money to deposit" it's not the case but I'm just saying.

She gave a crooked smile, as he pulled out from the parking spot, with the top falling to a resting position.

The radio started up, and he had XM radio, an old school favorite came on. It was Lodi Dodi by Slick Rick and Doug E Fresh.

"Lodi Dodi we likes to party, we don't cause trouble we don't bother nobody, we're just some men that's on the mic, and when we rock upon the mic, we rock the mic right"

Tamika would get excited over some old school hip-hop. She asked Terrence "what you know about this youngin?"

He said no better yet, "What you know about it?"

They laughed, returning to the days of when they were about 14 years old.

"Old school hip-hop is the best" nothing compares.

"True that sista, true that."

As he continued to drive they just listened to the tunes, and enjoyed a trip back in time, thinking about what they were doing at the time when a particular song came on.

Terrence didn't share as many stories as Tamika because most of his involved getting into some young girls panties, even as a teen.

He was feeling her though. He said she is cool as hell, and that smile when she laughs, he just wants to kiss her.

Tamika was hoping she wasn't sharing too much of herself, but she was relaxed. She was surprised the "date" got off without a hitch.

23

Terrence arrived at TD bank downtown on Montague Street. He asked Tamika did she want to come in with him, and she said "No". You realize you are double-parked right. He said that's not a problem. Tamika decided to wait in the car, and try to hold off those nasty traffic cops should they come around before you come out the bank.

"That is nice of you, sweetheart". I shouldn't be that long.

He said he wasn't worried about a ticket, but Terrence sure did not walk slow on his way to the bank. He opened the doors and there was a line to meet with a teller. He would have to wait because he wanted this money to clear his account by tomorrow. If the money was deposited at the window they would post it against the funds he already had in his account. He was planning to withdraw $5,000. A bit of it would go towards his household expenses, but he took out the rest to try and impress his new lady.

Terrence felt a vibration in his pocket. It was his cell phone. He took it out.

"Hello"

"Hey, what up man?" "Ready to get it poppin tonight? It is Friday we can party like every day on repeat, living up to the super star status we on."

"Nah, Ant I can't" not tonight.

"What "trick" you got up your sleeve? Or should I say on your arm?"

"Man, I'm chilling with a new lady friend, Tamika from the club last night, and don't talk about her like that" this one is different.

"Yea, ok Terrence" this is me, Ant, you talking to.

"Where are you at anyway?"

"I'm at the bank" I'm cashing half of the money from last night and going to leave the rest in my account, with the rest of my money.

"Speaking of money homey, I need a loan, about 2 g's" I have fallen behind in some things, primarily rent, and they may evict me. I have tenant/landlord court in 2 weeks.

"Not my problem man." Sorry.

"What Terrence, so you mean to tell me you would let ya boy get evicted?"

"I keep telling you, you are a grown man" act like it.

"I am taking out this cash to take care of my responsibilities and to see if Tamika may be interested in doing something nice with me, maybe for a weekend or something"

"Terrence, it's supposed to be Bro's before Hoes, you would spend money on a chick before helping your brother?"

"I saw this friendship changing a long time ago, but I had no idea how deep it went"

"It's cool though" said Ant.

"Are you coming around the way tonight?"

"I just told you I'm with my lady friend."

"Well, you must have forgotten there was a get-together at Dash's house" Drinking, Dice, Cards, you can still come through and bring her because you know it will be other girlfriends for her to talk to"

"So how about it?"

"Ok we might come through for a hot second but we not staying." I will text you, or maybe not when I am on the way"

"Cool brother" Ant said in a semi-angry tone. Not liking how Terrence has cast him aside for a woman he barely knows. "Bye".

"Lata" and Terrence hung up.

The line was moving he had about three people ahead of him.

"Beep, Beep" A text now came through on his phone. It was Tamika.

"I turned your hazard lights off, and I moved the car slightly down the street because the cops came, so I had to move, hurry up"

"Thanks" he replied <Send>

He thought to himself she telling me to hurry up like I control the line.

24

Terrence made the deposit. He stepped out the bank, and looked for his car. He saw it down the block and did a quick sprint to it. When Tamika saw him, she scooted back over to the passenger side.

Before he pulled off, he asked her did she have anything in particular she wanted to do today.

Tamika said, I told you "I'm rolling with you; whatever you had in mind is fine, really".

"Ok" well a friend is having a card game in my old neighborhood, and I would like to take you and show you off, I had to throw that in there because you are breathtaking. We don't have to stay long but it is in Canarsie projects, and I don't want you to be alarmed if you see dudes hanging outside, smoking, drinking and such.

"Let me tell you something" I am all the way 100% woman. However, don't get it twisted, I keep it street too. I'm not above it, and it's not beneath me, I just don't kick it in the hood like I used to anymore. Well let me take that back I still like to get my drink on, go see some of my peeps still there, sometime. When I was younger, I used to hang out in Marcy projects, with the people Jay- Z used to run with, so how you like that?

"Wow" sexy and a bit ghetto, girl, you wanna get married?

"Sure" after I have my lawyers draw a pre-nup, I know men like you, think they getting what I worked hard for but I got news for you.

"Now, I'm not saying you a gold-digger, but you ain't messing with no broke chick." Switching up a little verse from Kanye on ya.

And the laughter continued. Terrence started the car to drive off, he said let's go back to the bar and grille near your place, and we will continue to talk and become familiar until we head to my boys house later.

"Sounds like a plan to me" Show me the horsepower on this little baby.

Terrence said "you want me to get a speeding ticket?"

Thought you weren't worried about it, Tamika reminding him of his ticket comment earlier.

"True that, true that" it's just that I don't want to give you too much too fast, ya know.

"Yeah whatever" you scared it's all good. Tamika smiled.

Back to the bar for drinks they went.

25

As Terrence and Tamika were spending the whole day together having a great time, his boy Anthony was around the way doing the unthinkable. His "friend" had dissed him for the last time with their last phone conversation. Anthony and Terrence had been friends for over ten years, as of late that didn't seem to mean anything to Terrence anymore, how Ant viewed the situation. He was concocting a plan to rob Terrence of all funds, jewelry, or valuables he had on him when he showed up tonight. If he didn't show tonight he would just seek out another opportunity. He already knew from what Terrence mentioned earlier that he had about five thousand on his person. If he brought that new "Bitch" that was the final nail in the coffin that drove a wedge between them, then she is gonna get it too.

Anthony had jealousy that had been feeding off his negative thoughts for a couple years now. He let it get the best of him and he wasn't thinking rationally. He made a few calls to the local stick up kids, stating don't do them any physical harm but he told them it would be some money in it for them if they did this quick and in a hurry, and didn't make a "mess"

He wanted Terrence to be robbed as soon as he got there, because he was sure since he mentioned they wouldn't stay long; Terrence would leave before the house party got in full swing.

The "Stick-Up kids" Raz, and Celo, said they wouldn't hurt Terrence because they knew him, but business was business. Ant had told him if they got the full five thousand then they would get $500 each and the remaining four goes to him, since he put them on to make money in the first place. Raz and Celo were small timers; they probably would have done it for a pack of cigarettes and one hundred dollars each.

They are to hang out in front of the building with the other hustlers, acting normal, when they see Terrence coming they are to pull out their Ninja hole ski masks and run up on them once the elevator comes.

The plan seemed full proof and Terrence would be none the wiser. He would never think that he would get robbed in a neighborhood where he is known. Ant would have the money for what he needed, would still pretend to be his friend, and may even forgive him for making him go to such drastic measures in the first place, just to get by.

26

Terrence and Tamika talked for hours back at the bar. They drank quite a bit, but stopped right before they crossed the threshold of being drunk. They were "nice". If they were each with their mutual "crews", they would have kept going but they pumped their brakes. They didn't want to rush the evening.

Tamika let Terrence in on her past relationships, which she guarded. Let the past remain in the past was her motto. Terrence asked questions, she answered feeling compelled to tell let him know, she didn't have angry black woman syndrome, she was open to the idea of them seeing one another, no baggage. She did say she wanted peace and happiness in her life; the formula was simple.

Terrence talked relationships as well. He was forthcoming stating he played the field a lot but was looking to settle down now, he didn't tell that his conquests were in the hundreds as far as women went, and twice this week he slept with two ladies he didn't care much about; but he said did she have to know everything? Of course not, this was only their first official date.

They talked family, work, friends, and everything you can cover under the sun, then night began to fall upon them, he asked do you want to get ready to go to my friend's place? It will be getting dark soon, so we can be on our way. You won't meet a lot of people because you know how we do, most won't show up until 10 or after 11. You will however meet some; "the earlybirds" meaning they don't work, so they probably been chilling all day. I will call and see if my two boys are already over there.

Terrence called Dre first. There was no answer; he went to voicemail so he left a message.

Then Terrence phoned Ant; he picked up so Tee told him he would be there in about an hour around 8p.m or so. Ant said cool, I'm already here so I will see you when y'all arrive. They hung up.

Ant wasn't really there yet, although he was on his way, he just wanted to give the impression that he was already chilling, having a good time. He called his two "business associates" and told them be ready for action around the period Terrence indicated.

The would be robbers were ready. There was no turning back now.

Tamika before our evening ends, I would like to know "would you like to go out again tomorrow"?

"Yes, I'd like that very much"

"I knew you were just playing hard to get last night scribbling your number in my hand"

"Boy, don't get cocky and make me change my mind"

"Ok, I will shut up now" let's be on our way. They exited the bar for the second time.

27

They were on their way to Canarsie housing projects, and were still enjoying the old school tunes on XM radio from earlier, so they just cruised to that. They gazed adoringly at one another from time to time.

When they arrived at the Project, they went around the back way to park the car in a rarely used parking lot. Terrence saw people staring when he pulled up, probably trying to guess who he was or just being nosey. Usually when he comes around the way he is driving his truck, and he never has a woman with him. That was reserved for late night hours at his house after midnight.

After parking, Terrence came around and opened Tamika's door. He extended his hand to assist her out of the car. She obliged. They began their walk to the building, which was in view but some feet away.

As they approached Raz and Celo had their backs turned so their faces wouldn't be seen, they pretended to be chatting it up, but had to wait for the other cats to say what up to Terrence so they could time their entrance into the building perfectly.

All included there were four dudes outside, and no one was to witness the robbery. With no way to get rid of the other two, the stick up kids didn't have much time to put their face masks on once they entered the building.

Terrence held the door for Tamika and they went inside. A ramp in the building that you had to walk up led way to the elevators. They pressed the button and waited for the elevator to arrive back on the first floor. The building was a high rise with 13 floors, with nine apartments on each. Dash lived on the 11th floor.

The elevator arrived, and no one exited, so Terrence and Tamika entered. Watching from outside the door began to close. The thugs entered, ran past to the staircase adjacent the elevators to make it to the third floor to press the "up" button.

Faces covered Raz and Celo made it before the elevator passed 3 and so it stopped.

They rushed in the elevator when the door opened and told Terrence:

"Alright you pretty muther-fucker" hand over all your money and jewelry. And make this real quick so no one gets hurt. You make a noise and I will splatter you brains all over this elevator wall.

"Terrence just do what they say" Tamika said.

"Yea, Terrence you better listen to your pretty bitch"

"Yall don't know who y'all are fucking with" Terrence handed over his watch, dug in his jeans pocket and handed over a fifty dollar bill. Tamika handed over some earrings and rings that is all she had because she left her clutch in the car. She didn't know the people she was going to be around and was smart enough to leave it underneath the seat of the car.

Raz kept counting the floors in his mind and said we getting close.

"Last time muther fucker you think this is a joke, we know you holding some real money" If you care anything about this bitch you better hand it all over.

"My dude take out your knife."

"What?" Celo gave a confused look.

"I said take out your knife"

"Nah, we not supposed to hurt nobody."

"Shut the fuck up man, and do as I say."

"Check his pockets" and sure enough they found an envelope with all the cash Terrence had withdrawn from the bank earlier.

"Jackpot" they made the score.

They were on floor 9. "Make a move and I shoot because I ain't got shit to lose, or be stupid and try anything and I will cut this bitch.

The doors opened on 11 and they backed out quickly, running towards the staircase.

Terrence looked like he was about to run after them, and Tamika jumped in front of him.

She said let it go, the doors closed, and they were headed back down to the first floor in total disbelief they just got robbed.

"Are you ok?" Terrence stepped in and consoled Tamika, putting his arms around her.

"I'm fine" not so much shaken up but mad. Situations like this used to happen when we were little, I'm like people still doing stick up's and shit? I didn't want you to try and play hero because you never know what the outcome would have been.

"You're mad and I'm pissed the fuck off" Terrence took his hand and banged it against the elevator wall. The dude said nobody gets hurt remember? He fucked up. It's some shiesty shit going on. I'm gonna find out who did this and when I do...

"And when you do what?" It's still not going to make our stuff come back.

Terrence started to tell Tamika shut the hell up, but decided against it. It's not her fault what happened.

"They got my five thousand dollars Tamika" He punched the wall again.

Five muther fucking hard earned dollars that I made! Me! Nobody else.

"Babe, I know nothing I am going to say is going to matter right now, but please try to keep cool"

"Let's just go to the cops, and file a police report"

"Did you not say earlier that you hung out in Marcy?" "We are in the damn projects Tamika!!" Police don't give a fuck about a "nicca" getting robbed, and for me to say I carried five thousand dollars in cash, which is highly unusual, and I'm black, you may as well carry me away and lock me up now because I am going to look like a suspect not a victim.

"No cops" he said.

The elevator arrived on the first floor.

Terrence strong-armed Tamika, taking her hand and forcefully pulling her out of the elevator.

This time no one was standing in front of the building.

"Someone knows something." I will get to the bottom of what happened.

"Come on let's go back to the car, and let me take you home."

They walked the few feet back to the car; Terrence unlocked the door and still opened the passenger side for her.

He walked over to the driver's side, got in and they were on their way.

"So are you going to tell me where you live or do you want to be dropped off on a corner?"

"I think by the nice time we had up until just now, that I have earned your trust just a little.

"I'm in a foul fucking mood now and I don't want to mess up what he had tonight so just tell me and I will take you wherever." Excuse my language.

"I live in DUMBO Terrence"

"Address"?

"147 Front Street"

"Got it"

"Front Street it is" and he headed in the direction of her place.

28

The positive energy from earlier was long gone. The radio continued to play but Tamika changed the radio to a comedy station to lighten the mood, trying to get Terrence to laugh she knew it was a long shot but she tried anyway.

"I love Chris Tucker's material from when he was on Def Jam don't you?

"It's aight" he quickly dismissed her comment.

There was an incoming call received through his car's Bluetooth. It was Ant, so he picked up.

"Yo man, where you at?" I was for sure you would be here by now.

"Man, I'm not coming I'm dropping my lady off and then heading home, I will get with you tomorrow".

"Everything aight man"? You sound annoyed, you got woman problems already?

"Now is not the time Ant, now is not the time." I will hit you up tomorrow.

"Aight man, hope everything aight" Catch ya later.

"Peace"

The call disconnected.

Ant was on the other end smiling; the plan was carried out hearing Terrence's demeanor on the phone. He hadn't seen Celo or Raz yet but knew they should be making a drop soon. He was about to get the money and head back to his house, but not before showing his face by Dash's for a little longer to make sure he covered his bases.

Tamika noticed it was obvious Terrence didn't want to talk but she had to ask him a question.

"Terrence, I don't want to further upset you, but why in God's name would you be walking around with that much cash on you?" Do you normally do that? I'm not trying to get in your business like, how much money you got but five thousand? That's crazy.

To answer your question, "No Tamika, I don't usually do that" I took the money out because I was feeling you so much today, I wanted to ask you to go away with me for the weekend, not sure where, but you wouldn't have needed to pay for anything. I do well for myself with work, and the prize last night was the highest that I've won, but I do my thing on the night circuit so it wasn't nothing for me to take that money out if you would allow me to spoil you.

"You did that for me?"

"Yes I did"

"Oh my goodness, I don't know what else to say" except now I feel horrible because if you weren't doing it for me you would have left all that money in the bank.

Terrence said never mind all that. Don't give it any more thought.

"This shit is going to nag at me, but no need in you worrying too, ok?"

He said "Ok?" waiting for a reply.

"Ok" she agreed. I won't talk about it unless you do.

"You know you passed the house right?"

"Oh shit I did"

"You knew we passed your house two blocks back you just wanted to chill with me longer"

"Not with that stink ass attitude you got going on right now, no thanks"

"Ok, let me not joke, I know you not in the mood as you told your boy"

"Make a right here, and then another right at the light go back down two blocks and then make another right and we will be back at our destination"

He followed her directions and then they were in front of her building.

He double-parked and got out to open her door.

Tamika spoke first. "Terrence, I am sorry about tonight, but I must say I am not sorry about last night"

"What are you talking about?" Terrence asked.

"I'm talking about us meeting, I am not sorry about that." I had a nice time this evening, and I hope to see you again, I didn't think I would be smitten so soon.

"Well the feeling is mutual baby-girl" Let's make a date to do something tomorrow, breakfast first, something, since it's the weekend.

"Sounds like a plan" with that Terrence put his hands around her waist, pulled her in close and they kissed. A kiss they were both satisfied with; she slowly broke away from him and said "Goodnight"

"Good night sweetheart" Terrence did not move until he saw her enter the building and he knew she was safe. When she was out of view, he got back in his car to head home.

29

Tamika once she entered her home didn't waste any time getting Stacy on the phone.

"Girl, I have got to tell you, I had an awesome time tonight, I got jacked in the projects but that's not the point" Terrence is a gentleman, I may initially read him wrong.

"Wait, hold up, you had a nice date but you got robbed?" Stacy was thoroughly confused.

"This man robbed you and you are on the phone with me?" "We need to call my brothers to handle this!" A.S.A.P.

"No, Girl" Ok, let me back up. We spent the whole day together, mainly at the bar and grille and we talked for hours, he had an errand to run, I went with him. It was to the bank, he was walking around with a large sum of money, he decided to go see some of his friends in the projects and someone, well two guys robbed us.

"I don't know girl something smells fishy" You sure he wasn't taking you there to get you robbed?

"And how would that have benefitted him?

"I don't know girl" I'm trying to make sense of what you're telling me. So did anyone see anything?

"Nope, no witnesses" You know how it is in the projects hit or miss. There could be tons of people out in front, back or in the halls or sometimes it looks like a ghost town.

Anyway getting back to the date, I really, really like him, and he called me his lady tonight.

"Already huh? Don't you think this is moving kind of fast?

"Girl you know I am usually careful, with my screening processes", and look where that has gotten me in the past.

"I am thinking to do things a little differently this time around." And I am following my gut, I think he is being genuine with me. In fact, the money he withdrew; five thousand dollars was because he said he was going to ask me to do something with him one of these weekends all expense paid. I just needed to show up.

"He is going in hard, pulling out all the stops I see" Sounds like game but you old enough to make your own decisions and if you feel like this has the potential to go somewhere I say go for it.

"Thanks girl, I appreciate the support"

"I am your shoulder to cry on, laugh or whatever, but if he messes up" You know the rest…

They laughed.

"Yes, I do girl" I know the rest. All of us has let a brotha know at one point or another you mess with one you are messing with all of us.

"Amen to that"

"Well I just wanted to give you a call and let you know I am home, and I will speak with you more tomorrow."

"Good night girl" they both hung up.

Tamika, keeping her phone in hand, decided to send Terrence a quick text.

I know you may not have arrived home yet, if we put the negative aspect of today aside, then everything else was truly special, hoping you have a good night and we will talk tomorrow. <Send>

Tamika went into the bathroom to get out of what she had on to take a shower, and get ready to lay down for the night.

30

Terrence was mad as hell about the robbery. He was home, and decided he would call his boys tomorrow before meeting up with Tamika to see if they heard anything. He checked his phone and saw the message from Tamika and all he could muster was sending her a text saying:

"Sweet dreams, and more to come my Angel." <Send>

Terrence knew he wasn't going to get much rest. He wanted to go back by Canarsie, and question every dude he thought he was cool with, the ones he wasn't cool with, grandma's, kids, or anybody he came in contact with. He decided against it because he knew, just as Tamika said it wouldn't change anything. The projects have a no snitching rule, so what's done is done.

"Five thousand dollars" he said to himself again. "Fuck!"

He would try to get whatever rest he could and tomorrow is another day.

31

Terrence didn't need to call Dre first thing because word had gotten back to him about what happened with the robbery. Dre phoned Terrence around 9a.m., and asked could he come over. He had just finished visiting his grandmother in the nursing home, so he could pass through on his way back to the house. Terrence said fine, he was already up anyway.

Not long after their phone conversation there was a knock on the door. Dre had arrived. Terrence went to the door and let him in.

They gave each other a pound, and Dre proceeded to walk into the living room. They both were seated.

"Man I am sorry about what happened to you last night" I didn't even wind up going to Dash's house. I saw the missed call from you this morning; Ant didn't call last night, but I had a couple of missed calls. I did some overtime at my job, and when I went home and showered I fell asleep watching tv.

"But yo' another one of the missed calls I had was from Bub", he said it's all hearsay of course, streets are talking, he heard my boy got robbed, he had like twenty thousand in a duffle bag, and if he come around there again whoever robbed him is going to get whatever he holding again" Call him back.

"I didn't even call dude back because I didn't want to feed into it more, you know what I'm saying?" Plus, I hadn't even talked to you.

Terrence sat across from Dre listening attentively to all he was saying to see if he was a part of this or genuinely for him. He didn't trust anybody now.

"It's just crazy man" I told you when I called before, people had they eye on that pocket change you made from the moment you won. I'm telling you people don't think no more they just act. You got something people want, they see an opportunity they just take it. I'm not just talking about you, that could have been any one of us last night. Then Ant was going around telling everybody that y'all got that money, y'all are superstars, this and that. He just needs to grow the fuck up because he knows he don't live the life he bragging on, but I'm not here to talk about him, I just wonder what the hell he be thinking sometimes.

"Are you alright man?" you need anything? Dre asked.

"Na, I'm good man" Thanks.

I didn't sleep and been going over things in my mind, but it's like something is missing. So Ant was running his dam mouth again though? I don't know why he keeps thinking what's mines is his. I'ma have to distance myself from him for a bit. Cause right now with what you telling me I feel a need to ask him why he was running around the projects telling people what we got, when that nicca can't even pay his rent.

"That's your boy" said Dre.

And don't take this the wrong way Dre, I may not holla at you for a while either. I need to get my head together, plus I met this shorty that I'm really trying to get to know. No games this time, and I'm dead ass serious. I owe it to myself to talk to the fella downstairs in my pants and tell him I am controlling this one, and he needs to play the background.

"Wow so you gonna tell your "Johnson" he can't come out and play for a while?" "You not gonna try to get no ass?" I gotta see how this unfolds. I know you talking about falling back but you better keep me posted, I haven't seen you serious about a chick in like forever.

"Hey man, I need you to do me a favor"

"What's that?" asked Dre.

"I need you to put the word out that we spoke if anybody else calls you about what happened tell them someone dropped dime on who it was, and I'm gonna see them". They don't have to know it's all bull but that will make the rats scurry. Someone will talk and when I find out who it is, I can see what I want to do about it at that time. I'm going to let everyone talk, wonder where I'm at or up to when they don't see me, trust a "nervous "nicca" is the worst kind because he always gonna be looking over his shoulder.

"Yea man no doubt, I got you" If I do hear anything else worth telling, I'ma holla as soon as I do. Just keep ya head up man, I know you took the "L" on the loot, but more will come your way.

"I'm bout to get up outta here, I got stuff I need to do today, and I want to hit the gym."

"I'ma get with you"

Aight Dre, I'll be in touch.

Dre was up and headed towards the door, Terrence followed and saw him out.

32

Terrence took a minute for himself. He walked to his room, sat on his bed staring at the wall. Rather than continue staying upset or feeling sorry for himself he decided to dial up Tamika and see what she was doing.

He called and she answered.

"Hey babygirl, how are you?"

"I'm doing okay, more importantly how are you doing?"

"Better now that I am talking to you."

"Aww that's sweet"

"So what do you have planned on your agenda for today?" I know you wanted to get breakfast but I understand if you are not in the mood to do anything, we can meet another time.

"Actually that's why I was calling". I want to see you, and I need you here with me. If it's not too much to ask can you spend the weekend with me?

"Um, I know you in pain upset or whatever, but I'm not sleeping with you."

"Tamika, Tamika, cut it out already with this defensiveness" All I asked you was to come over and be with me, we can talk all night if we feel. I have a sofa bed in my living room, and three guest bedrooms, so you do not need to sleep with me.

"Again, I'm sorry, I jumped to conclusions" I can come over and chill with you this weekend. You give me your address and I will drive over. I will also bring some movies; do you like ROM-COM's?

"I like some, like Love and Basketball, or Love Jones"

"I am more of a horror flick dude though" The more gore the better.

"Ok well, I will bring a few from home, and on my way I can stop and pick up something from Blockbuster"

"Pick up Paranormal Activity" I don't care which one I missed the last two. I would also like to see Resident evil if they have it.

"Ok those are embedded in my brain"

"When would you like me to come over?"

"The sooner the better, I'm home, and just waiting on you."

"Ok, I will get dressed and be along shortly" but first I need that address.

Terrence gave her the address and directions to the house so she was all set.

33

Tamika arrived at Terrence's place. When she first entered, she was amazed at how large it was. A single man with all this room, he owns this home in Brooklyn, yea this man is making some serious money she thought. Not that she wasn't handling her business, but that did make him slightly more appealing.

"Here let me get your bag for you," Terrence said.

"Thanks" replied Tamika.

"You're looking lovely as always"

She replied thanks again, and asked so are you going to show me around?

"With pleasure."

As they walked around the house, it was a multi level, he had a den, an unfinished basement, a gun collection, which surprised her, he didn't seem like the type to take interest in that. He also had walk in closets, which she truly admired; she envisioned all her clothing fitting nicely in there.

They finished the tour and went to relax in the living room, it was the afternoon by now but still rather early. Terrence excused himself and decided to go into his bar and make them some Mimosa's.

When he returned Tamika asked "you moonlight as a bartender on the weekends"?

"I have a lot of skills babygirl"

"Mmm hmm" I bet.

He handed her the drink, and he said let me propose a toast. "Sometimes you don't have to know a person forever, to know that it's forever" I hope this continues to grow. Toast to you my special lady. They clanked their glasses, and took a sip of their drink.

The day continued for the two, as it would for anyone who appeared to be in a relationship. They talked a great deal, family was a big topic; what type of relationship they had with their parents, how their life was growing up, and even shared painful childhood memories they had buried. Not only had they found a confidante in one another, they really appeared to be soul mates.

This continued throughout the weekend, they watched movies in between talking, ordered take out for dinner; and come Sunday morning Terrence made her breakfast while she was still asleep.

They never officially said they were a couple but in a matter of a few short days they both knew the other is whom they wanted to be with.

When it came time for Tamika to leave Sunday evening, it was difficult for the both of them. She had her overnight bag in her hand and before she spoke, he said you can leave that here you know..

"She joked are you sure your other girlfriend won't mind?"

"I'm sure" there is no other. Those women before you those were diamonds of a lesser class, they had clouds in their stones, but you dear are of the highest quality you are an "E class" the best there is.

"Alright Romeo" I'll leave it here. I just wanted to tell you thanks for not rushing anything, and making me feel very comfortable with you. You are a real dude, unless I am having a bad judgment in character right now, I think you are cool, and a real man. That is rare to find.

"Tamika, stay with me don't go home"

"We have work tomorrow"

"You can leave early in the morning, in time enough to not be late"

"We can sleep in the same bed, and don't have to do a thing" I just want to hold you.

"Alright, I will stay" in her mind she was glad he asked.

She told him, no funny business, my reflexes are quick and I would hate to "accidentally" knee you in a sensitive section.

"Yea I would hate that too" He gave a half grin; joking about his manhood was not funny.

"Well I'm going to get showered" you can use the other bathroom if you want to freshen up, and I will meet you in the bedroom.

"You are the man with the plan"

Terrence carried her bag back in the house from by the door, and he went towards one bathroom and she went towards the other.

They met back up in the bedroom, she was wearing a cami-set, and he didn't wear a shirt just his boxers, they both took a deep breath before they got in the bed, but it was lights off, turned on her side, he came closer did the same wrapping his arm around her, and they attempted to fall asleep.

It was "hard" but they both managed to get some rest and find comfort in one another's arms.

34

Morning came, Tamika got up early enough to leave head home to change and then on to work. Terrence was still sleep, so she didn't disturb him.

Tamika locked the bottom lock from the inside and just pulled the door closed behind her.

She did in fact make it in to work on time. She was tired from getting up earlier, and today was a busier day than normal, because her job had poured tons of money in advertising to garner new business and clients, and it was working. Tamika had tons of financials to mull over and help people with their investment portfolios but she was a pro at what she did, stress and all.

Tamika daydreamed about Terrence all day long in between trying to remain focused.

The day was moving along since she was thoroughly engrossed in work. She decided only to take a break, since she didn't have lunch with her. Stopping for a moment to phone chat she put an "Out to Lunch" sign on her desk so she wouldn't be disturbed.

First, she called the girls and did a conference call; she knew they would have some time to talk for a minute.

Conferencing Stacy, Ann, and Jackie you heard all the Hey's, Hello's and what's up simultaneously on the line.

"Ladies I was calling to see if we could get together for dinner tonight?"

They all were free; but Jackie asked, "What's up?"

"I can't meet with my girls just to see them?" I didn't need a reason before, I don't need one now.

"I know what this is about" Stacy said.

"Do tell" the other two said.

"I think Mika gave up some bootie this weekend"

"There you go assuming and no I did not"

Let's go to BBQ's on Livingston Street and meet around 6:30p.m.

"We all get off regular time so that will work."

"See you all then"

"Yes, see you, bye."

Tamika decided to place another call to Terrence, she hadn't heard from him today.

After the phone rang several times, he answered. He didn't seem to happy to hear from her, his "hello" was rather dry.

"Hey babe" why are you sounding like that? Tamika asked.

"I'ma keep it real with you Tamika." I don't like how you got my head all messed up. I got up this morning looking for you and you were gone. No good bye, no text, nothing;

I thought we were headed somewhere but I guess that was only how I was feeling.

"Look at how you got me whining like a little girl right now." All that was missing was leaving some money on the nightstand like Robin Givens did my man Eddie Murphy in Boomerang, and that would have been us. "I feel so cheap."

"Boy are you done?"

"Yes I am"

"Babe I thought about you all day today" I didn't wake you because you were sleep, and I didn't text, that's my fault but I'm calling you right now. "How are you doing?"

"I'll live"

"Wow, you a drama queen too?" Who would have thought not the mighty Terrence.

"So am I going to see you later to make up for what you did to me this morning?"

"What do you have in mind Terrence?" I'm going to meet my girls for dinner, but after that I'm free. If we don't see each other this week. I am on vacation next week. I told you I had some scheduled days off.

"Stay with me again tonight" he said.

"I can come over after I'm done with dinner, I wasn't going home after work, but I have enough time to go get some of my things, and still be on time to meet up with them"

"So I will see you tonight then?"

"That's a yes, Mr."

"Shoot, look at the time; my break is over I will talk to you later Hun, smooches."

"Have a good one he said" and with that it was back to work.

35

Tamika had enough time to run home after work, and meet the girls at the restaurant. They were already there when she arrived having Daiquiris with an extra shot of Rum. They were talking about their day and the weekend so when Tamika sat they jumped right into it.

"So I've already filled them in that you have been kicking it since last week with the dude from the club, and that's all that I said" Stacy was talking.

"Well give us some details" the girls were all waiting.

"I guess tonight is all about me huh?" I missed the dirt on your ladies so now I gotta tell my business. I'm kidding; but what can I say? He's handsome, generous, gentle, we like some of the same things; writing, old school music, and most of all, he seems genuine. Yes, for the past few days we have been heavily wrapped up in each other. In fact I am going to stay with him again tonight at his place.

"Again?" asked Ann and Jackie.

"Yes, we slept in the same bed and nothing happened"

"Now that's a first" said Jackie.

"Maybe for you" said Ann because you are used to giving it up on the first date.

"Ladies, c'mon enough already" Not tonight, please.

"So the only thing I will say, is I am going to be spending a lot of time with him" He already calls me his lady, and said I am the only one, so I guess I now have a boyfriend.

"Translation to us, I am going to spend a lot of time with him, and less time with us" said Ann.

"I want all of us to be happy in our lives, and that includes love life." If I have to devote some time to see how this develops that is what I am willing to do; but if this doesn't work out, well "I just don't know" we'll have to see, with this man I am not even thinking that way now. Therefore, I expect you ladies to be understanding, just as I would be if the situation were in reverse for any one of us. I will still be in touch stop acting like I am going to forget about y'all altogether. My girls, my sisters, you all, I will never forget what you've done for me, and offered support, no man can supersede that so don't even trip.

The waiter came over and asked the ladies did they want to order anything else. Tamika placed a drink order, and shared the appetizers already ordered. They were going to hang around the restaurant a while longer, and then they would each head home for the evening.

36

Tamika arrived at Terrence's house later that evening. She was tired. It had been a long day.

He greeted her at the door, as she had texted him and let him know when to expect her. When she walked in he gave her a single rose, and also had rose pedals on the floor leading to the bathroom. He had drawn a bubble bath, and had candles lit, where she could just unwind. It's like he knew what she needed without her even speaking the words. She gave him a tight hug, and followed the path to the bathroom.

"All this is for me? She asked.

"No, it's for this other chick I am waiting on so you better make it quick" They laughed.

"Wow, Terrence" This is just what I needed. Thank you.

Tamika paused as she thought about what she was about to ask.

"Would you like to join me?

"Nah, you go ahead and enjoy your bubble bath" I have something else waiting for you once you get out the bathroom, so go ahead and relax.

Tamika thought, ok is he gay? Turned me down; but keep your mouth closed just go soak in the bathtub.

She stayed in the bathroom for about 30 minutes, and when she emerged found him waiting in the bedroom. He had candles lit there too. He told her come lay on the bed. She was again wearing another boy short cami-set like the previous night, this time she had her long hair out. He motioned for her to lay on her stomach. He reached for the massage oil he had on the nightstand and began to massage her shoulders. His touch felt so good to her. He continued to massage her back, underneath her cami, her arms, took her hands inside of his and twisted her wrist, until she was so relaxed her hands felt like jello. He went down to her legs, and the back of her calves. Little pleasure moans had escaped that she hadn't intended for him to hear; but he did. That brought a smile to his face. Tamika was aroused, and wanted to go to sleep. She had to decide which one she was willing to commit to tonight. She decided to sleep with him, she wanted it, he wanted it, even though she knew he was trying to take his time with her. She assumed he wouldn't think this is something that she did all the time so she said "what the hell" and went for it.

She turned over from her stomach to face him so he lifted up off her, when he saw she was moving. She said you lay on your back. He did what he was told.

Tamika asked him was he open-minded? He replied "yes" with limitations depends on what you are talking about…

So she decided to go a step further and asked…

"Terrence do you trust me?" and he again replied "Yes"

Only wearing a pair of cotton pajama pants and no shirt his six-pack was again on display tonight.

She looked over on the table with one of the tea-light candles and carefully picked it up.

"He said what are you doing?"

"She said Shhh."

She took the candle and poured some of the hot wax on his chest, he screamed, but once he got used to it, he let Tamika have her way. She put the candle down, and went to kiss his chest, gently brushing away the dried wax chips. She then ran her tongue up and down the center of his chest. He liked what she was doing. His manhood was penetrating through his pajamas. She pretended to lean in to give him a kiss and then went for his neck, his body was so sensitive all he could do was curl his toes and laugh.

She said "What's the matter?" Can't take it?

"He said I can take it but I can't wait any longer to have you" While she was kneeling on the bed he slid from under her, and they both met in the center of the bed, now face to face they kissed passionately. He took her cami straps and slid them off her, and went to kiss her breasts. He took his hands and massaged her garden through her boy shorts. She was dripping wet. He laid her down on her back so he could make love to her.

She stopped him and asked, "Do you have condoms?"

He said "In the draw next to you there should be some"

Tamika checked and there was only a single condom remaining.

"I guess we will have to make this count"

He said "I guess so" Now come here. He grabbed the back of her hair as her head was tilted; he licked from her chin down to the center of her breasts. Since they were already well into the foreplay Tamika opened the condom, and slid it on his manhood. He entered her, and it was so "tight" because it had been a while, and thanks to her kegel exercises, felt like she was a born again virgin. The satisfaction they both felt while making love, was beyond what either could have imagined. They both climaxed, Tamika went to the bathroom to dispose of the condom in the toilet, and to freshen up. She also brought a washcloth to the bed to clean Terrence; both drained they fell asleep in each other's arms.

37

Morning came, and this time Tamika, woke Terrence as she was leaving. She drove her car and did not have to leave as early as before to go to work, but she noticed she leaves out before Terrence nonetheless.

He pulled her back on the bed said "Good Morning and give me a kiss"

"She said not with that morning breath you got going on"

He said "Oh, it's like that"

"Yea it's like that babe"

He kissed her on the forehead, and told her have a good day. He asked will I see you after work today?

She said you know it.

Later when we meet up I am going to have something else for you.

"I hope it isn't a surprise like last night, because that could get us into trouble."

"That's the trouble of the best kind sweetheart, but no it's not that, or maybe that will follow, I don't know" When you come over you will find out.

"You have sparked my curiosity, but I have to be on my way"

"I love you"…

"I mean"…

Terrence, I didn't mean to say that it slipped out. I just wanted to say have a good day. Tamika couldn't get to the front door fast enough before he had a chance to respond.

She felt like an idiot, how could you say that after a few days together? I will have to face the music later this evening or maybe he didn't hear me. Maybe I am over thinking this. He probably didn't hear those three little words. Tamika was standing on the outside of the door on his steps, but decided to move her feet now and get on to work.

38

Everyone at work was busy from the moment they walked in and watching the clock until 5 pm comes. This was the first time where Tamika didn't want her workday to be over due to the events that happened earlier this morning.

The day was full of meetings and administrative duties like any other day but it went by too fast for her.

It was approaching 5p.m. but Tamika did not want to see Terrence. She texted when it was 5:30 and said she would be there within the hour; he texted back ok.

When she got to his house she rang the bell he let her in. There were no rose pedals around so it wouldn't be a repeat of yesterday. He did tell her come in and have a seat.

He said first, I bet you worried today because you said you loved me this morning. Well Tamika, I love you too. So don't think it's not reciprocated. I never felt like this before.

Tamika opened her mouth to speak, and he said let me finish.

He said the surprise that I have for you are keys to my house. You don't have to move in with me because you just bought your own place, we are not there yet; living together. However, since we are going to be seeing a lot of each other, I want you to be able to come and go as you please, that way you know I am serious about you. So there you go the keys to the castle. I also have something I want to say to you, and it goes a little something like this…

Dare I say,
From the way I've played,
That Terrence has finally found a woman of substance,
Because I just knew from my encounters,
A woman like you simply didn't exist
But what did I think I would find amidst,
A pool of immature women,
Feeding an ego of an immature man,
That's why I toyed with their emotions,
Because they couldn't relate,
They just couldn't understand,
That a man needs more,
He has more to give,
Always depending on a man,
Get your own life to live,
But I saw independence in you,
And what you would bring to the table,
Tamika within you,
I know that you are able,
To love me,
Yet love yourself,
You are your greatest asset,
But with you in my life,
I now know wealth,
We are going to walk together in this thing called life,
Today as my girlfriend,
Some day in the future to become my wife.

"Pick your lip up off the floor he said"

Tamika was speechless. She said do you mind giving me a moment?

He replied "Not at all."

She took her bag which; also had her notebook in it and pen; she wanted to scribe something to him that would thoroughly express how she felt, or at least a response. She was in the bedroom at this point with nothing but silence around her. She blocked out the noisy Brooklyn streets, or the people yelling in it, and wrote, "How I feel"…

All I knew were nights and darkness,
Afraid of what would happen,
If sunshine were to combine,
With some inkling of hope,
In this hollow heart of mine,
Then by chance,
We of all places met at a bar,
And have been inseparable since,
Well at least thus far,
You're taking a chance,
So am I,
The stars aligned properly,
And I still wonder why,
But Terrence, you saw something in me,
Those previous men seemed to toss aside,
I cannot run from you,
I cannot hide,
I am thankful that love you have for me,
That I can reciprocate,
Together,
 On our wonderful journey

She called him into the bedroom, and recited that to him. He said "thank you beautiful" and they hugged.

39

They continued seeing each other consistently for months, going on romantic dinner dates, trips to the park, and even went on a cruise to the Islands together. Terrence splurged on Tamika like there was no other for him. He brought her an expensive tennis bracelet, matching necklace, and other items "just because" he knew his Angel would appreciate the gesture. She felt secure in the relationship overall but began to have her doubts, as certain situations arose.

There were a few occasions where Terrence's time was unaccounted. She went to the office to surprise him for lunch, but he took an extended one, and his cell was off for hours. Even after office hours, he returned home late, and rushed to take a shower. His excuse was that it was a business meeting, and it didn't matter if she couldn't reach him every minute of every hour of the day. He was very defensive when questioned about it.

Then there were times when they would be out at Luke's which was now their "spot" and two women on two separate occasions gave Tamika the stare down like they wanted to scratch her eyes out. They addressed Terrence with a flirtatious hello, and didn't acknowledge that she was sitting there. His not introducing her did not help the situation either. Terrence noticed her irritation, and laughed it off as if something was funny. Tamika had a feeling he knew those women on a personal level or they were ex's but she could never get him to speak on it openly like he had when they first got together. She felt disrespected, but he brushed it off; because in his eyes, he was treating her as his woman, and she had better remember how good he has been to her.

Then there was the lovemaking, at first it was tender, loving and protected. Now Terrence insisted on not wearing condoms. Tamika was against it at first because she knew they weren't married, and that safe sex is the best sex. Against her better judgment, the condoms came off numerous times, and Terrence even talked about getting her pregnant. She was on the pill so she just let him talk. She knew that she was not having a baby with a period of under a year dating, and "if you like it then you should put a ring on it" Thanks Beyonce. The kicker to the lovemaking was that it became infrequent, or sometimes when he would orgasm; not much came out as if he drained the pipes already.

Things were up and down, mainly up, but they did get into their share of arguments as well. Terrence felt that although he still loved her very much, she was becoming a nag. His eye had begun to wander from time to time, and he began to resort back to his old way of thinking.

There is nothing wrong with getting an escape from the pressures of home with some outside loving. Terrence was not about to break up with Tamika, but he didn't want to have to deal with all the headache or responsibility of home right now. Therefore, he cheated a few times with random chicks that he met when he went out solo. There was no way he was going to let Ant, or Dre know his business since they know he had been kicking it serious with Tamika

for a while. He wasn't about to hear their I told you so's...
"You can't commit to anyone." At the end of the day, they
don't care about his being committed or cheating; they just
loved proving Terrence wrong.

Terrence's indiscretions amounted to going to hotels
because he couldn't take the women to his house, and one
chick still lived at home with her mother. Another woman
invited him over but she had three kids, all under the age of
five and after the second encounter with the kids knocking
on the door, crying and running rampant, he decided he
could no longer see her. The condom came off the second
time, he decided that April was not worth his time, and he
did not want to become one of her future baby daddy's.

Tamika had taken notice to Terrence's behavior and she sat
him down one day after he had come home from work. She
said we need to talk, and he said ok.

She got right down to it no beating around the bush. First
order of business, question number one, "Are you happy?"

He said "Yes"

Question number two "Are you cheating on me?"

He answered "No"

"Where are you going with this line of questioning,
Tamika?"

"I'm so glad you asked Terrence"

Let me tell you one thing, what I am not is a fool. I know
you have dipped out on me on at least one occasion, I knew

about it, sat on it and asked myself could and would I forgive you.

"But how did you?"…

"Don't worry about how I know; but you would be amazed who sees what when you are leaving places that you are not supposed to be" And don't worry about trying to lie to weasel your way out of it, I am past that.

When I thought it through, I said "yes" because I figured you were having a lapse in judgment, and you would come to your senses. It's also not to say that I haven't thought about it myself, but I haven't acted on it. You know how many fine men would like to date me? A lot, let me just put it that way. So consider this a fair warning, that if you cheat on me again or if I find out about it we are done.

Terrence didn't hear the most important part of the conversation that they would be over. All he heard from the conversation was she had thought about cheating too. To think of cheating on Terrence Jackson she has nerve! This woman is crazy! I'm going to keep an eye on her.

Tamika just used the ultimate psychology on Terrence. She had no inclination of cheating; but she knew a man like him would never be able to handle his own treatment being done to him so she planted a seed; just the way for her to get her point across. I may still be here and love you, but you are not going to just walk all over me. She knew from day one when she met him he had a bit of arrogance about him, so the way to get through to a man like that, you have to humble him and go for the ego.

They were finished with their talk. Terrence asked Tamika to go with him to the video store to rent a movie for the evening. She laughed because as busted as he was she thought that was fast, the dog trying to get out of the doghouse within five minutes of a talk now knowing where he stands. Had she not had time to process this beforehand, this cheating situation would have gotten him busted windows on both his cars, possibly more.

40

For the month following their talk, Terrence was home everyday how he should have been. The sex was almost back, to where it was, and he was as attentive as ever. It seemed they were rekindling their friendship; learning how to treat each other with the respect, they had in the beginning, although everything happened so quickly.

Then it happened, about two weeks after his month of good behavior, while at home; which has mainly been Terrence's place, Tamika received a phone call from a blocked number. It was a woman that claimed Terrence and her had sex. She said a few days ago, he didn't go to work and was with her. Tamika asked what her name was, and the woman replied "it really doesn't matter, because this was a one-time thing" Your man is a dog, and he treated me horribly, it's like he just wanted to get it, and after we were done he wanted to run as far away from me as he could. She went on to further explain they met at a pizza shop in Brooklyn on Fulton street months ago, but he had not given her a call until recent. She said this cell number popped up while he was in the bathroom, and it said "wifey." So she jotted it down real quick to see if he was in a relationship still, and then you answered.

"So are you his wife?"

"You have a lot of balls calling my phone with your number blocked you damn coward, asking me questions on the nature of my relationship with my man!" Let me make sure I got this straight, he fucked you and then left you high and dry and now you're mad and you want to warn me? Well let me thank you the Brooklyn way, "Bitch don't call my phone no more with this bullshit" If you do I promise it will be the last call you make, and hung up on her mysterious caller. The phone did not ring again after that. Tamika must have put fear in the heart of that woman.

"I can't believe he went and did this shit to me again!" Fucking men! And this one was good, he really had me fooled, thinking he loved me. Well Tamika, talking to herself, she said you know what you need to do. Get your shit together, the main stuff you will need, and just leave and don't look back. You've been through worse shit than this and survived, and will get through this as well.

Tamika feverishly gathered her things, and had everything she needed where she would not need to see him again. She decided to leave a note on the bed though, one of his favorite places he would be sure to find it.

Terrence, thank you for proving I was right about men like you. You say one thing out your mouth but your actions show another. I got a call today and you must have thought I was joking when I said if you screw around on me again, I was out! You just can't keep your dick in your pants can you? Do you really have to be with so many women? You know what, I am not going to make this long. I got my things, everything I need, so do not call me again, and if you do, you won't reach me because I'm changing my number, and if you come by my house I will have you arrested for harassment. My heart was not to be toyed with, and you did just that. So I hope whatever the bitch name was that called me and snitched on you when you

were supposed to be at work the other day, it was worth it!
Have a nice life bastard!

You fucked one,
You fucked them all,
I took you back,
But sex remains your downfall,
You think I need you?
No I don't,
To get this good loving,
Now you won't
You got you a hoe,
Now stay with what you got,
You blew the last minutes of the game Terrence,
Because I was the winning shot!

The copy of the keys that she was given was on the bed
next to her note. Although she felt horrible, and
heartbroken she somehow felt she was leaving with dignity.
Spared the pain of the drama because he was not home yet;
she grabbed her belongings, and headed to the door and
never looked back.

41

Terrence realized he messed up. He did everything in his power he could to win her back. He was able to leave voicemails on her work phone, because she made good on her word and changed her cell number. She never listened to the messages, just automatically deleted them. He never did go by her house because he really believed she would call the cops on him, and he did not want to get a record over a relationship, well cheating or harassment, whatever she would tell them.

He sent flowers to the job everyday for three and a half weeks' straight, with different love poems attached. The poems were discarded, but Tamika saved the flowers until the end of the week, and had someone from the local hospital come pick them up and give them to patients who were terminally ill, or needed a boost in spirits.

He tried to reach out to her friend Stacy, but that proved to be pointless the one time he called her she started yelling at him on the phone he knew he didn't have an ally in her.

Terrence figured he could go to her job, and see if he could catch her when she was leaving, it was a long shot but one worth taking. She said she would call the cops if he came to her home but not the job.

He showed up before 5p.m and waited outside 30 minutes until she appeared leaving the building. He called out "Tamika" she saw him and kept walking. He ran up to her. He said "Tamika, Mika, please hear me out" I am so sorry I hurt you. I didn't just hurt you, I hurt myself because now I don't have you.

She kept walking to her car and said do yourself a favor don't come here anymore. Forget you met me, as I'm trying to do the same. Time heals all wounds or so the saying goes, so I'm praying that it's true. "One thing your dumb ass said that was true is you don't have me" Now grow yourself a pair, and walk off in the other direction in which you came. I got a life to live, and it doesn't involve you.

"Ok, Tamika I am going to grant your request" but I won't stop wishing that we will one day get back together. I know we were meant for one another, even though we'll be apart never give up on the thought of us, alright?"

Tamika was at her car, she closed her door, put the key in the ignition, and began backing out of her parking space.

That was the last they saw of each other for months....

"Cocktail for Disaster"

Part 2

42

Leaving the restaurant, I decided to wait in the lobby as it was pouring outside. Another evening alone, Am I destined to live the single life forever? Why are my expectations so high? I told myself a million times if I don't expect anything then I do not leave myself open to disappointment.

As I pondered these thoughts, a hand pierced the back of my neck, slightly cold the embrace felt quite familiar. I should have been startled but I wasn't. I knew it was him. After more time passed I secretly hoped for a run in; and like he said from when we last saw one another, I did not give up on the thought of us. I had to work past the hurt and anger. When and if it occurred I wasn't sure what I wanted. Scared to turn around I closed my eyes to inhale the manly fragrance that made me warm inside and moist between my center. Is it possible to start over? In my mind I had to "get a grip."

He turned me to him saying "Ms. Mika", "Been too long, you looking good girl"...God has answered my prayers running into you like this. A higher power has intervened and this is the opportune time to talk to place all our cards on the table. It starts with tonight no games, and no strings. I am going to be forward and say, if taking a step towards me as a man and what I have to offer is not enough for you, then continue to stand, watch the rain pour outside, and I will be on my way. Just know, I have changed.

Motioning more towards Terrence, I stood there looking like I've seen a ghost. Tamika say something, I said to myself, but no words formulated. He on the other hand was still talking. If you choose not to come with me right now, we will both be left with regret. So what's it gonna be? Haven't we hurt one another enough simply by being apart?

I communicated with a half smile rather than take the time to make my decision because no room was left for thought. He stated his intentions and sometimes the best form of communication, was to say nothing at all. I was ready to hear him out (again). I extended my hand for him to lead the way out of the restaurant. He looked downward and breathed a sigh of relief. We stood there for a second, like are we really about to do this? Talk; leave together? After so much damage, is there anything to salvage?

"Ok, so we are ready to roll." Here is the plan, I will go get my car, and you come outside once it's in view. He took his jacket and placed it over my head; opened the door and was gone. Time stood still, but when the car approached finally made its way in front, I decided to toss the jacket. I now exited through the restaurant doors. Feeling uninhibited by the rain and empowered by the events about to go down, I simply let the rain caress my body. Nipples erect and standing at attention, he rolled the window down and said what are you crazy? You're going to get sick that's why I gave you the jacket for protection. I started laughing almost feeling intoxicated, but no alcohol was giving me this feeling. I said protection. Protection who needs it? In my mind, I said could it all be this simple. "I'm not making any sense, just get in the car."

The ride was a short one, and one in silence. I don't know if it was the sexual tension between us, or if it was the butterflies I was feeling but I know I couldn't wait to get to his house.

43

Nearly 15 minutes after arrival, and still driving around that was enough. I asked for the keys to his house so that I could go inside. You would think that if you could afford to pay $1600 monthly mortgage you would have a garage, but then again this is NY, The Big Apple, some luxuries you are not afforded and a garage was one of them; therefore, continuously around the block he would drive. He said he would be right up, soon as he found a parking space. That wasn't a problem because that would give me time to freshen up.

I got out the car, walked up the stairs, and went inside. Damp, the rain felt sexy on my caramel skin. I wanted to be touched oh…did I want to be touched. Not only touched physically but mentally I want to find security in the arms that have held me many a nights.

I opened the door to darkness. Sliding my hands across the wall for the light switch, I found what I was looking for. I hung his jacket up on the coat rack in the hall, and stripped down to my matching bra and thong. I didn't waste any time, and here it is we're supposed to be talking. I was right on point with my Victoria's tonight, and that's no secret; I'm looking PHT, translation: Pretty,

Hot and Tempting. My next step was removing my clothes from by the doorway. Bending over to scoop them up, I stood in awe on my way back up.

The clothes immediately fell back on the floor. Terrence had taken the time to redecorate by painting it the color I suggested, not to mention purchased the antique furniture I picked out of a house and home magazine. The walls filled with memories of our pictures that we have accumulated from our whirlwind romance. He also had a wilted rose on the end table.

There was a noise at the door, then it unlocked, it was Terrence…. He entered and I told him looks like he has been busy these last few months; undressing at the door he said appears so. His eyes showed he wanted to take me right then, approving of what I was "not" wearing. I walked towards him sliding my hand across the wall to the light switch to dim them, so we can be more comfortable. Helping him out of his attire, as it seemed he was having difficulty, I grabbed his tie and asked, I did a quick inspection and I think what you did with the place is amazing; however one thing does not fall into place for me. What is up with the wilted rose? After all this decorating you mean to tell me you couldn't afford a fresh bouquet of flowers?

He said isn't it a woman's job to make mental notes of everything? The rose, this long stemmed old Rose was given to you coincidently ten months ago on this date, "I see you forgot about that". I gave it to you saying your love is like this rose beautiful to behold, yet delicate to the touch. I kept the rose for what it represents now…my heart that has withered away since you have been out of my life. You know we walk around thinking that whatever we have today it will be here tomorrow. Sadly enough we know this as truth although it is not, refusing to change certain aspects of our lives until it is too late. I know I hurt you by telling you one thing, and my actions showed another. I should have let you know as a man that love frightens me. Your love frightens me. It came into my life at a time when I needed it, and it was so powerful it took over my thoughts, my entire being. I never experienced love in that capacity before. You by my side were all I needed, I now realize.

Having had my share of women, and I mean alot of women… Terrence started to go left a bit so I slapped him on the shoulder, and he caught focus of what he was attempting to say. Damn I'm sorry, caught a flashback. I frowned, wanting to walk away..

Look Tamika,

"Mika, sweetheart" I was just playing.

Ok, ok "I'm sorry."

I should not have gone there, but seriously, I want you by my side as long as you'll have me. I know you still love me, and I love you, everything about you. Then came the silence again…just when I decided to seize the moment leaning forward to give him a kiss he held up his index finger and said "don't move".

He went over to the stereo and put on Luther Vandross, "If this world were mine". He knew how much I loved that song. Pulling me to the leather sofa, motioning me to lie on my back, I complied. My feet hung on the floor, as my upper body lay flat on the sofa. He placed his hands on my thighs, and began to massage them up and down. His hand movements extended up to my breasts while massaging my nipples through my bra; gradually intensifying as he softly placed wet kisses on my belly button and in between my thighs. I slowly started to arch my back as he began to tease me. I told him I didn't want him to stop talking.

"Why don't you speak your other language, the one where you talk with your tongue between my legs?"

He started to smile and asked the dumbest question.

"You want me to go down on you huh?"

I laughed, "you seem to be a smart man, do what you feel."

He asked "what are you going to do for me?"

"We'll have to wait and see" keep any requests in mind for later, we have all night.

As he neared my face, I closed my eyes. He softly traced my lips with his tongue, and blew a soft gentle breeze across my lips. He parted my lips with his tongue and I took him inside my mouth. We kissed and kissed growing hotter with every single moment. As I continued to lose myself, something did not feel quite right. Trying to stay in the moment, I realized why we were not together…

It is because of his ability to make me lost in the moment and then hurt me the next; always apologetic, yet repeating his mistakes. Now although I was feeling a bit overwhelmed, my mind was just uneasy at this time. Again, something is nagging at me, is it because I'm not supposed to be here or because of the fact that I am?

I needed answers. My subconscious took over my thought process. Terrence did not notice the change that was happening within me. He continued to deliver all the attention to my body that I so badly wanted and should have been enjoying.

I tugged on his ears, pushing him back some, indicating stop, and he asked, "What are you doing?"

I said "Be patient sweetie, slow down, you're going to get yours tonight.

"Babe" Go to the basement and get me a drink, please.

He looked upset that I cut into our session and said "now?"

"Now is a good a time as any."

I'd like some wine from your assortment of liqueurs. I needed to numb my senses and calm what was brewing inside of me. I had all kinds of emotions and thoughts running through my mind from one extreme to the other.

Besides, I know he becomes more talkative when he drinks, let's see if I can get the real Terrence to come out to play, not the smooth talker who doesn't hang around long. He returned with three bottles of Pinot Grigio, and complimenting glasses. He wanted to make sure I wouldn't ask him to get up again anytime soon at least as far as drinking was concerned. I told him there was no rush to get me into bed; although I'm the one who started to seduce him. I reminded him earlier he said he wanted to put his cards on the table. I was all ears. He must have forgotten that part because his face grew blank. I knew about the women he had cheated with so what else could he possibly need to place openly discuss?

He used the corkscrew to open the first bottle of wine, and poured us up a glass. I drank as if it was water. Before he could set the bottle down on the table, I extended my glass "refill please."

He said "Wow."

Just like the night we met when I bought you a drink. "You're thirsty huh?"

"I guess you can say that." "Afraid you can't keep up Mr.?"

"Oh no, I can keep up with you, Ms. Tamika, and then some."

He poured up a second glass. Before you go devouring this one, I would like to propose a toast, "Here's to second chances".

"Yes, second chances."

He leaned in to kiss me on my neck; he knows what that does to me. I allowed him to proceed with kissing me again because I said as long as we drank I would keep the upper hand and get the information I wanted.

We drank and drank some more in between fondling each other, and as I filled our glasses with the last of the wine from the third bottle, which didn't take long to empty, I started feeling more sexual again. This was not the plan, I was supposed to have the level head, but both of us were buzzed.

In a soft, loving tone, I said c'mere and "get what you've been missing."

Let me make you feel good handsome.

"No" that's my desire towards you, it's your world. After laughing because of the fact that we were disagreeing about who was going please who, we got in the sixty-nine position.

Kissing, licking and passion ignited too late to stop now…

Ready, I lay on my back and spread my legs so he could have a good look at my wet black box. I was 100% in, aroused and stimulated. He penetrated me. He took long, slow strokes, to make me gently moan. We both neared climax, I needed this to last longer and I wanted him deeper inside. Time for me to be more aggressive, I flipped him over, or what was an attempt to flip him over with his assistance, he on his back, I began to ride him…

"I've always loved you Mika."

I'm in my zone now looking him in his eyes swerving those hips. He spoke…

"You will always belong to me." I was trying to finish before my concentration is broken and I miss my chance at the big "O"… a few more strokes…

"Here it comes"…

"Yes, Yes, Yes" Big Daddy, I screamed in ecstasy.

Our union cemented, we collapsed in a pool of sweat. I was tired as hell because that was quite a session. As we lay next to each other, he continued, what I was trying to say is…

Terrence "Shut up." "Savor the moment and give me a second." "I was not listening to you with all your emotional talk a moment ago, because it's not the dirty talk I had in mind." "You know what I'm saying?" "Man up babe, man up."

This is important. Never mind you with your newfound drunken-gangsta persona. I'm the man and I am going to say as I please, and you are going to hear me out, end of story.

"Now" I know I am a selfish man. I wanted everything when I already had it. You were all those women I cheated with wrapped into one.

I wasn't trying to hear this after what we just finished. This is not pillow talk.

Did he just speak on his past flings? I was all of them? Very slowly, I tried coming back to reality. Or was I? I was confused. I just wanted to get dressed, leave and accept this for what it was a night of sex.

I got up to begin gathering my things and he asked "what about us?"

You just said I was all of the women you cheated with rolled into one.

I mean c'mon "Are you serious?"

"Of course you are" I answered my own question. That's classic arrogant Terrence, no surprise there.

We broke up for a reason, and no matter how things can correct themselves for the moment; things will not get better at this point. That's just the stage we're at nowadays. I knew my speech was slurred but that had to make perfect sense.

Obviously, you didn't hear what I said while you were trying to fuck the shit out of me a minute ago so, let me repeat myself. Apparently, his alcohol not having as much of an effect on him as it did on me. He was speaking very matter-of-factly.

"I love you."

"I'll always love you."

"You can't leave me when you already belong to me, forever."

"Dude you sound like a crazed stalker." Remember I told you that in the beginning too? I really think it's true now.

I knew I needed to get out of there quick; our session was quickly going from nice to insane.

"I'm not done."

"I got a call from April, Tamika."

Frenzy slowing a bit; he had my attention. April was the next to last female he cheated on me with some months ago.

"Why would she be calling, she wanted another booty call?" Sarcasm intended.

"Go give her what she needs."

He replied "No" that is not the reason.

Her test came back positive, and she was inclined to let me know as I have been adversely affected from that day.

"Test?" "Affected?"

"You lost me"

Is she pregnant? You're the father?

"No" Ok, Dam!! Can I finish? Then maybe you won't have all of the questions.

She's HIV positive and suggested that I get tested.

"I found out that I too, am HIV positive, and there is a good chance that you are also."

I froze and shouted "Oh My God" we just had unprotected sex.

"Tell me you took the test and you're negative."

"This isn't happening." It's not happening, as I took a seat and rocked back and forth on the sofa.

The plan I derived once we started drinking, to get him drunk and open up caused me to be careless which I rarely am. We had a few occasional slip-up's in the past but nothing I thought I needed to be concerned with. My life began flashing in front of me.

"It's the alcohol, I'm tripping."

"I'm still drunk, high, something."

"Now repeat to me what you just said Terrence." Clearly, I misunderstood you.

"I know you did not say you are HIV positive"

"You didn't misunderstand Tamika."

"You heard correctly." I am HIV positive, and you are at risk. I contracted it while we were together when I had unprotected sex, with several women, but the disease was confirmed by April.

I dropped to the floor crying. He knelt down, cupped my chin in his hand, smiled and with no remorse said "Cheer Up, I'm positive", but guess what we will be together forever.

"You sick bastard"

"What the fuck are you talking about?"

"I knew if we had this conversation prior you would have never wanted me."

"I said you damn right."

Now you have no choice but to stay with me. Everything is going to be o.k.

"Be real with yourself."

"You know you had no future without me honey." I took care of you, and since we've been separated you have done nothing to further your life, indicating you need me.

I gave a cold, empty stare. I felt my soul leave my body. Like an out of body experience if this is what it would feel like. He wants to destroy my life and everything I have worked so hard for, including happiness; not going to let him.

Think Tamika Think.

I put on a smile, got up and said "you are so right"

We're perfect for each other. I am always going to be with you.

"Baby will you excuse me while I go freshen up?" You gave me a lot to process.

"Look at me I'm a mess."

"Sure, but don't take too long, sweet thang."

"I won't"

"Now that's the Tamika Grace, I know and love"

This is just a minor setback for us, not the end of the world. I want to go another round now that we have cleared the air.

"Whatever you want" I will be right back.

44

I found myself bypassing the bathroom and continuing down the hall to his unlocked gun collection in the den. One of his favorite pastimes besides screwing other women will work to my benefit. He likes to build rifles. He also has small handguns to display when guests come over. I chose a Smith and Wesson M&P 9mm. It's easier for me to handle than the Glock17. Oh, I know a thing or two about handguns, trust! Terrence took me a few times to the shooting range for some of our dates. How ironic to suffer at the hands of your own weapon and acts of selfishness. Gun in hand I was now "locked and loaded." One clip with 17rounds makes me an extra 15 shots dangerous. I am not trying to kill him just severely injure him to where he will want to die. He wants to go another round? The only round he is going to get is the one I'm about to unleash. Sick bastard would probably still cheat on me and infect other unsuspecting women. I have to make a move now before I lose my nerve. This isn't a well thought out plan, but nothing about tonight has made any sense.

I made an about face, walked a few steps in the opposite direction and halted once I reached the bathroom. I needed a towel to conceal the gun.

I called out to him from down the hall; "Baby where are you?"

"Over here" right where you left me; where else would I go?

He was lying on the floor still naked, calm as can be.

"Baby", remember when we first got home and we were getting uh, familiar again? You asked what am I going to do for you?

He said" hell yeah" and I could tell he was smiling.

"I'm ready" close your eyes. The wait is over.

"This is gonna be awesome, I know how you love to please your man"

"Eyes closed, you gonna tie me up too you freak?

"No, not this time, are your eyes closed?"

"Yes"

I was so light on my feet that he didn't hear when I was right up on him. I nudged him to open his eyes to the sight of black steel in his face. He immediately cowered against the couch, but there was nowhere to go.

"Tamika" put the gun down now!

"What the hell do you think you are doing?"

"I don't think I like your tone Terrence" and besides you are not in a position to make threats and hand out orders wouldn't you agree?

"I am just trying to get you to realize this is not what you want to do."

"This is not you Tamika, you are not thinking right now."

"I will forgive you just please, put the gun down."

"You are too damn funny, you know that?"

"You will forgive me" "You will forgive me?" I yelled.

"Was I the one to give you this potentially deadly virus?"

"You really got it twisted." And I have been so good to you! I even took you back when I first found out that you cheated on me, when you were claiming to love me so much! What an idiot I was!

Terrence inched closer as he thought he had a chance to grab the gun.

"Ah, ah ahhh" I wouldn't try that if I were you. The safety is now off; any sudden movements could be detrimental to your health.

"Of course if you want to speed up your process to the grave let me know"

"Actually, I think you are ready for the grave." You walk around here like you are "God's gift to women." When you are the lowest form of human being there is.

I'm going to put you out of your misery for all the pain you inflicted on me and the potential others. He made a sudden movement.

"Pop!" One shot went off to the chest.

Tamika, "You shot me"

"Call 911."

"Please" I am begging you.

"I may call in about, oh, let's say 2 hours, does that work for you?"

"Tamika, this is serious, it's not a joke." "I could die."

He was holding his wounded chest and the blood quickly turned his hand deep red.

I told you not to move Terrence; but you never listen. You always do what you want, never once thinking about the consequences. I loved you, I really did, and you hurt me. Even after you are no longer here, I have to find a way to deal with this.

At this point Terrence was crying, and making a final plea not to do anything else.

"I love you too Tamika". "Believe it or Not" you were the best thing that ever happened to me. I never meant to hurt you. If you call 911, I will not press charges; I won't even tell anyone that you were responsible.

"Shhh" Terrence enough talking.

You know why my mother named me Tamika Grace?

"Of course you don't so let me tell you" You have time for a story don't you?

My dad was the one settled on the name Tamika actually, as soon as he knew he was having a girl. He just loved the name Tamika. He said he thought of Meek. The definition: having or showing a quiet and gentle nature. My mom on the other hand thought more of her pregnancy itself and said it was smooth; I gave her no problems before or after my arrival. I was such a blessing to my parents. She said through life starting from the moment she held me that, I was covered with "God's Grace." Therefore, that is where my name is derived from.

"God's Grace" Hmph.

If only mother could see me now, well I know God is watching but I feel more like Tamika "Fallen from Grace".

Blood was now covering the floor. I stood there frozen not realizing I had it in me to pull the trigger.

I aimed at him again, this time he wasn't begging for his life anymore. I pointed the gun at his leg, and fired off another shot. Since I was at such a close proximity, it tore a chunk of his flesh off. There were bits of blood and skin all over.

He screamed in agony, winded, crying, and appeared to be trying to get something out.

"Tamika" We don't always do what's right, I'm the biggest person at fault here. Sometimes people don't walk in a straight line, and love is not black and white you bitch. "You don't get it do you?" I am Terrence to the Mutha Effin Jackson. Ha Ha! I'm not going to have fear cause' this blood is pouring out my body. You want an apology? Not going to get one; I am just saying I see where I drove you to getting a gun, and shooting me. Unless you have the balls to finish the job…We still gonna be together, because once you get tested, and I'm sure I know what the results are going to be, whose gonna want you? Look at how you reacted tonight. You don't handle shit well at all; but we still gotta move on from here.

"You hear that Tamika?" His speech slowing, but he still kept talking. It was apparent he was weakening from the blood loss.

"Sirens"

"Shit"

"Shit is right"

"You're going down bitch."

"You sure you want to start talking shit now Terrence?"

"Are you absolutely sure?" I aim the gun at his head this time.

Out of all the days of the year, your neighbors decide to be home tonight.

"You're saved by the bell."

"What's the matter Terrence?"

"Looks like someone is in pain and still has the nerve to have an attitude" For a person who stated they wouldn't press charges, who wants forgiveness, your actions are not matching your words. Even when faced with death you will never change. You still want to be in control.

"I started to kill you" but I can't bring myself to do it. You are right; this is not me. NYPD is probably on their way to your door any minute now.

"I wanted to run" Bury your body in a deep hole, and keep moving.

"I don't know what I've done."

"You've won, Terrence." You always win. More than likely I'm going to jail. I don't even know my status, but you've broken down the stability of my mind. It didn't just happen tonight. I was getting over you and putting "us" behind me, but you managed to take me through the motions again and weasel your way back in. That is on me, when I saw you again and knew to walk away and didn't, I have to live with that. I don't know what's the silver lining going to be in all of this, but may God be with us both.

45

"Boom, Boom, Boom" NYPD came banging on the door.

"We got a call of reported shots fired"

"Is anyone inside, is anyone injured?"

"Hello"

"Boom, Boom, Boom." The knocks louder than before.

"Yes, Yes" Someone is injured. Someone does have a gun.

"Me; Officers" I said talking from behind the door.

"Officers" listen to me carefully.

"Can you hear me?"

"This is Officer Robertson."

"I am his partner Officer James"

My partner and I can hear you just fine.

"Is this the Assailant?"

"I am no assailant" My name is Tamika. Terrence and I are the only ones in this home. He is wounded, and has been hit twice. There is quite a bit of blood, and his breathing is becoming faint. He is on the living room floor, and you will see him when you come in. I was armed however; I am placing the gun down, so do not come in here shooting.

"Ma'am we have our guns drawn for our protection" We are going to need you to unlock this door right now, so things do not escalate to worsen the situation. We also need to be in there so the Medics that are waiting outside can tend to this Terrence individual you mentioned. EMS has responded to the scene. "Ma'am"…

"I am coming to the door"

"I have no gun remember" Unarmed black woman, unlocking the door.

Terrence did not make comments thru any of the exchange between the police and I. Looks like death may come for him after all.

I placed the 9mm on the floor, as I stated I would. I then "clicked" the first lock on the bottom; that was opened. As the second and final was unlocked, the police immediately pushed the door in causing me to fall and hit my head.

One Officer rushed past to tend to Terrence, Medics in tow, and I became acquainted with Officer Robertson, he handcuffed me while I was down, stated the charge and began reading my Miranda rights.

"You are being charged with Felony possession of a firearm and the intent to commit serious bodily injury, which will be upgraded to murder if this man dies." This is due to your confession through the door.

"You have the right to remain silent. Anything you say can and will be used against you in a court of law. You have a right to an attorney. If you cannot afford an attorney, one will be appointed for you."

"Get up"

"On your feet" Do you understand these rights as they've been read to you?

"Yes"

"Now what went on here?" Do you care to elaborate more on what you were saying through the door?

"I have nothing to say to you without my lawyer"

"Ok, Ms. Tamika" I will be escorting you to the 77th precinct for processing.

"Robertson" his partner called to him.

"Yea, James what's going on with the victim?"

"He is naked, sustaining a gunshot wound to the chest, and one to the leg" The bullet exited and reentered his leg, but at the site of reentry it was nearer to his femoral artery. It just missed it by several inches. The Medics..."

"He's in critical"

"Coming through, Excuse us" They rolled Terrence past us on a gurney. We are taking him to Kings County Hospital. Appears he is going to need a blood transfusion. We were able to stabilize him, but it can go either way at this point. "Let's keep rolling." Just like that the EMS workers wheeled him out.

"Off to the precinct we go."

46

I was escorted out of the home, with my head held down in shame. The officers draped an oversized hooded sweater on me that was on the coat rack in the hall, which is all I have to my name right now. Yellow tape was being placed around the home, as we made our way out the building. Other officers arrived on the scene, taking photographs, and setting up to gather whatever evidence they need for this case. Neighbors were watching, Camera phones were flashing, and videos recorded as we came down the stairs. Not the type of attention you want to be known for. If this turns out to be a media covered case, I'm sure there will be someone on TV stating "Things like this never happen in our neighborhood" or "She seemed like such a nice girl." We reached the cop car, and he opened the rear door. He placed his palm on top of my head and indicated for me to bend down slightly and get in the vehicle.

This was my first time being in the back of a police car. It was my first time being on the opposite side of the law too. If what I know from TV is correct, I am going to be allowed one phone call. Whom will I call? Stacy? Jackie? A Lawyer? I forgot my purse at Terrence's. I don't have any identification, I guess I won't need it where I'll be going. Maybe someone will bring it to the precinct. That is the least of my problems. I continued thinking random thoughts. Everything happened so fast, it's unsettling all the things going through my mind currently.

The cops didn't say anything to me during the ride. I bet they are making all types of assumptions too. It's their job not to assume, just stick to the facts. Not that they have a lot to go on considering I did not explain thoroughly what happened; but I bet I am the jealous girlfriend, stalker lover, etc. If Terrence lives, he should actually go to jail. I may have pulled the trigger on the gun, but he assaulted me as well. Assault with a deadly weapon, that dam virus he is carrying around in his system.

We pulled up at the 77th. The cops got out and left me in the car for a few minutes. When they returned this time, they escorted me into the building.

"My temporary housing is ready boys?"

There was no reply. We walked straight through some sliding doors. Passing several desks, more Officers of the law, and inmates, we arrived at a desk where I was told to have a seat. The two officers that escorted me; were conversing with another Policeman, off to the side, who looked of higher authority than they were. As they wrapped up the conversation, Robertson sat, James left, and the other Officer looked like a Sergeant of sorts.

"We are going to need to go over a few details." First Tamika state your full name, address, and date of birth and social security number."

"Tamika Grace, 147 Front Street, DUMBO, Brooklyn, July 4th, 1977, 258-08-1372." I wasn't calling you DUMBO by the way officer, you do know that DUMBO stands for "District Under the Manhattan Bridge Overpass."

"Thanks for clarifying, I'm aware." I am noting on your paperwork that said person did not have any contraband, except weapon that was retrieved from the scene of the crime, valuables, or medication. Now you will be moving to a holding cell until our Investigator is ready to get your fingerprints and photograph. I will be checking for any outstanding warrants. Follow me. The other high ranking officer left to stand over another officer's desk currently with a suspect there. I guess he is paid to monitor precinct business.

We walked further towards the back. This is where the actual holding cells were.

"Officer will I be able to make my phone call?" I am only entitled to one, correct? By the way, I do not have any warrants. I'm not a criminal.

"No, that is incorrect; you are entitled to three phone calls." You will receive notification when the time arises for you to place those calls. Checking for warrants is part of procedure, and everyone in here is innocent until proven guilty in a court of law. Your day will come to tell it to a jury of your peers. You have declined to give any details to me; the arresting officer at the time; therefore, it is important that you wait until your lawyer arrives, from here on out we are prohibited to further discuss anything with you.

"Halt." This is your cell.

"Officer" I have one other question.

"By any chance would I be able to get a pen and a piece of paper?" I can write what I need to in front of you if the pen would be considered a weapon.

"We do not honor such requests Ma'am." Let's remove your handcuffs. Now proceed to enter your cell.

"Isn't it too early to have a roommate?" My question went unanswered, as the door slid closed behind me as I walked to take a seat on the bench chained to the wall.

47

"This is your first time in lock up isn't it?" I can tell. Asking for amenities; I haven't laughed all day, but you got a chuckle out of me. I'm Tanya, Tee-Tee to the streets, and I'm in and out of here probably every other day. It's like the courts ask for me personally. Guess I'm what the psychologists call a Classic Case of not learning your lesson. Hardheaded, or, I have a better one, I am not breaking the cycle of dysfunction that is buried deep in my subconscious from when I was young.

"But who gives a shit you know?"

"You do what you have to do to survive." It doesn't change just because you have a badge, or live a certain type of life, like these pricks seem to think. They don't know people's circumstances. I look at them with disgust, like you don't know me; don't judge my life. The only one that I respect in here is Jazz. She's good people, and that's my baby.

"You know what I'm saying girl?"

"Why are you even talking to me?" I blurted out.

"I am happy to have someone to" ... Just because we are behind bars doesn't mean we need to act all stuck-up, I mean look where we are at. So back to what I asked "Do you know what I'm saying?"

"If I answer then will you back-off?"

"Yea, I get what you saying about people not knowing your circumstances and judging." I don't know anything else about your lifestyle, nor do I care to know "Sorry." For a moment I thought Jazz was a dude until you said she, and well, you're a she too. That's cool, you have someone to love, or love you back. I don't go that way, but I just agreed with you, no one wants to be judged.

"You know we gonna be in here some hours so we may as well talk."

"What you in here for?" "What's your name?"

"Tamika, and the rest I don't want to talk about now."

"Everything is still fuzzy." Things spiraled out of control quickly.

"Sometimes it's like that girl."

"You go with the hand you're dealt."

"I've been on my own since I was 14." I have been bounced around from foster home to foster home, molested by my Aunt, and her brother, yes my uncle. That's probably why I'm all messed up now. Neither one knew the other was forcing me to have sex with them. I despise men for what he did to me; so I never tried a relationship with one. He was drunk when he first tore my little womb up. He did it once, and got away with it telling me; your mother would be so angry at you if she found out what you've done. I thought he was telling me the truth. She was trying to get clean from cocaine, and I didn't want to be the cause of breaking up the family or a relapse. So I never spoke on it, until I did some time, and these courts mandated counseling as part of my sentence. I have animosity for my Aunt but there is something nurturing about a woman that I am drawn to. Guess that's why I identify as a lesbian. Took a while though; I am 30 now. I got a habit of stealing, because I feel like there can never be enough of anything in my life, so I try to compensate for that. "Sticky Fingers" that's me. That is why they know me so well around here. Jazz and I hooked up before she was accepted to the Academy, and she became a Cop. I knew her from around the way, before she straightened up her life. We used to run with the same crowds. Now she is busting some of the same people that used to be her friends. In life, you make choices. We just happen to be on opposite ends, but found something special in between. I don't even know why I blurted out to you that we are together because I have never done that in my entire life. I must be drawn to you. You give off this innocent vibe; non-threatening, even with the attitude and short answers. I don't know why you are in here, and I hope it's not serious. You'll find out when you get arraigned, and see the judge. Whatever you did if you get a slap on the wrist I hope I don't see you in here again, that's real talk. Doesn't seem like jail is where you belong. For someone like me, this is my second home.

"I don't mean any harm." I think you are trying to apply some of your psycho-analytical babble and project it on to me." I don't need you to figure out if I'm a devil or an Angel. A tortured soul, with a troubled past, or stole a piece of candy from the corner bodega. "I'm in here." That means I committed a crime. There was no mistake or injustice. "Understand?" It's been a long day. Going to be an even longer night, I just need a pen and paper to write a letter. I write it's how I cope; not by telling my life story to a complete stranger. I see what you are trying to do, but now is not the time. Maybe if we met under different circumstances, I would be that warm receptive person, you think you see. She is not here in this cell with you, trust me. Moving along to a different topic, or perhaps we can just listen to the other inmates in the other cells, we don't have to bond.

"I'm gonna ignore the fact that you tried to again get feisty with me." You must be under a lot of stress. So this is not going to be a walk in the park for you. I get that. You're lucky I got a soft spot for women. I'm not trying to come on to you either. I am however going to do you a solid. You didn't ask for it, but I got some under the table juice in here thanks to my girl Jazz, when no one is paying close attention to her actions and whereabouts, prepare to be amazed.

"Yo, Yo, Officer" "Yo, Poe-Poe" she yelled.

"I need some assistance"

"Can someone come to the cell?" I know you all can hear me.

"Officer"

"Inmate Tee-Tee" Where in the world is the fire that you are screaming back here to the top of your lungs. I need you to tone it down. Now what can I do for you?

"Officer Jazmine, I need to use the restroom." It's not for the quick one either, it's not a "one" at all if you know what I mean. Did you get my joke? Not a number one? Where is the humor? Where is the love for your model inmate? I crack me up!

"Step away from the prison bars inmate." I am about to open your cell door.

"Everything Ok back here Officer?"

"Yes, Sir" Just a bathroom break for Inmate Tanya, as I secure cuffs on her.

"That is fine" I came to get inmate Tamika. It is time for her to use one or all of her phone calls. Step forward inmate, we need to go back into the other area of the precinct. Extend your wrists, so you too, can be restrained.

"Walk this way" We arrived at an old school looking pay phone in the hall.

This inmate has one minute remaining on their call. They are timed; five minutes each. Once the line is free, you will remain cuffed, and since you were booked without a wallet or identifying information, you can call collect. If the call is not accepted that still counts toward your call limit.

One minute seems a lot longer when you are counting every second in your head as if your life depended on it. Mines did actually. The inmate before me was removed from the pay phone and I began to walk towards it. I picked up the receiver; my collect call was going to be to my attorney, Brandon Donaldson, of the Donaldson and Donaldson law firm in Manhattan. Please accept my call, it is after business hours, but he usually stays at his office late. I met him years ago when I wanted to fight a minor traffic offense. Since then I've had a few legal issues needing resolve, and he was the man for the job. I am not going to put my trust in legal aide. I've always said if I had a legal matter I would call him, and I've given him a lot of business by way of referrals. I pressed the number "0" for the Operator.

"Directory Assistance how may I help you?"

"I would like to place a collect call to the Law Office of Donaldson and Donaldson at 212-555-5609."

"Please hold to see if your call will be accepted" We were going into the third ring, when I knew by the fifth if no one picked up it would go to his answering service.

"Donaldson and Donaldson" Can I…

The operator interrupted the woman that answered. "You have a collect call from… Caller state your name… Tamika Grace." Do you accept the charges?

"Yes, we will."

"Thank you Jesus, Thank you God."

"Hello?"

"Hello, this is Patricia the Legal Aide for Donaldson and Donaldson" How may I assist you?

Again, this is Tamika Grace. I am a client of Attorney Brandon, is he available?

"I'm sorry, he is gone for the evening" May I help you or take a message?

"Yes, Please." I'm sorry to be rushed but I don't have a lot of time. I am in jail at the 77th precinct in Brooklyn. I haven't been arraigned yet, I am waiting for my paperwork to finish processing here. The Police are gathering information by standard procedure I suppose. I don't understand much of what is going on, it has not been further communicated because I refused to talk and cited I want my Attorney; so I am in the dark.

"That was very wise of you without legal representation you could actually do yourself more harm by speaking on your behalf." So what are the charges?

"I shot someone."

"Ms. Grace, do not say anything other than what the officer's charged you with."

"Something about possession of a firearm, and intent to cause serious bodily harm, the charges are not verbatim"

"So this was not Self-Defense?

"No, Ms. Patricia"

"I have a feeling I am going to spend the night here, and won't get to see a judge until tomorrow, or later." Please have Mr. Donaldson call the Precinct and let them know if he will accept my case, or be at the arraignment, and the officers will tell me. I am not contacting any family members or friends, for bail if granted. I will use my other calls to get in contact with the office if anything changes. I have money saved, spread over several accounts. Payment will not be a problem. I just need proper representation. My time is about up.

"Ms. Grace are you sure you do not want me to contact anyone for you?"

"Yes, I am sure" I want to spare those close to me as much as possible. They will find out soon enough when they do not hear from me for a few days they will think something is wrong and begin calling. I can have you contact someone if need be after we know what is going to happen to me.

"Time is up inmate." Hang up the phone.

"I gotta go."

"Bye."

"We will be in touch by…" I did not hear the remainder of what she said as I had to hang up on her. I'm sure she understood my position.

"That is the only call I wish to make"

"Then I will return you back to your cell."

Proceed to walk in the same direction in which we came; back down this hall.

A few yards and we were back.

"Stop" Here is your cell.

"Step away from the door, so that I may open it".

"Wrists please…cuffs unlocked, now, step inside"

"Thank you Officer."

48

The door slammed closed behind me. I just stood there. I may as well talk to the walls when I try to talk to these cops, because they don't utter a word.

"Welcome back Roomie" I was beginning to wonder what happened to you. I thought you were sprung or something. I took a few in that bathroom. Stomach was hurting you know.

"T.M.I, Okay" I let out a deep sigh.

"Hey, come have a seat" You didn't even notice the gift I left for you on our comfortable seating accommodations.

"What are you rambling on about now?"

"Uh, that's why I said come see"

I walked over to Tee-Tee.

"Where did you get this from?" I couldn't believe I was staring a pen and pad in the face. You could get in trouble for this; well even more trouble. Why would you go out on a limb for a stranger? For me?

"Girl, I think instead of playing 50 questions with me you start writing to whomever you want, or have your writer's therapy." I told you I have "sticky fingers". On the way from the restroom escorted by Officer Jazz, I swiped the pen and pad from her partner's desk. He isn't playing with a full deck so he will think that he simply misplaced it somewhere. Officer Jazz didn't see anything of course, she was "busy" fixing her badge, so she won't know how it got to us, and therefore has no sense of what happened.

"I don't know what to say except thank you" That's all I have in me right now.

"Thanks"

"No problem" Now get to writing, I know the pad is small but the smaller the better. Now if someone comes by particularly "Sergeant Nosey" that's the prick who checks to make sure everything is running smooth in this house, then you deny knowing how it got in here too, let them deal with the particulars.

"Got ya"

I began writing.

I am not sure whom this note is for but I need to get some things off my chest. It is probably an open letter to me, but in case this gets to family at some point in time, I just want to say I'm sorry. Sorry, I reacted inappropriately to my pain, and had a temporary lapse in judgment. It trickled downward, extending to each one of you that I love so dearly. It will be some time before we can put the pieces back together, and even then there will be "invisible scars" From the beginning, this situation rapidly turned from a sunny sky to an ashen existence. As I write from jail, behind metal bars and brick walls, my life is uncertain. The direction of life yesterday bright and promising is not that of today. A man is in the hospital somewhere between life and death, and we await the outcome. Funny thing about outcomes…Not everyone is built for the aftermath. What lies ahead as several lives hang in the balance? Right now, we play the waiting game however; we will have the answer soon enough…

Trials, Testing, and Tragedy follow in Cocktail for Disaster: Volume 2. Does Terrence recover from his gunshot wounds? How does Tamika cope with her actions and dealing with the news of her status if confirmed? Was any of this worth it? Stay Tuned for Volume 2, promising to be an exceptional read when the outcome culminates to an unexpected ending.

I welcome any questions or comments, and answer all e-mails. I can be reached at Stephanie@Onewomanenterprise.com

Thank you for your continued support.

~Steph The Author

The purpose of this book is to entertain as I previously mentioned, but also to bring awareness to the HIV and AIDS epidemic that is still prevalent today.

Many of us are still are not practicing safe sexual habits, increasing our exposure to potentially life-threatening diseases.

Please protect yourselves and be safe. A condom is a small consideration before that moment of "loving" that will benefit you, than to suffer an unfavorable situation/result later.

Check out www.aids.gov for more information on testing, resources, or possible support groups.

And, www.aidshealth.org for information also.

www.ingramcontent.com/pod-product-compliance
Lightning Source LLC
Chambersburg PA
CBHW070827180626
46818CB00001B/423